Wolf Hollow

Wolf Hollow

a novel

Lauren Wolk

DUTTON CHILDREN'S BOOKS

An imprint of Penguin Random House, LLC

DUTTON CHILDREN'S BOOKS

Penguin Young Readers Group

An imprint of Penguin Random House LLC

375 Hudson Street

New York, NY 10014

CIP Data is available.

Printed in the United States of America

ISBN 9781101994825

10 9 8 7 6 5 4 3 2 1

Edited by Julie Strauss-Gabel

Design by Irene Vandervoort

Text set in Harriet

For my mother

Wolf Hollow

PROLOGUE

The year I turned twelve, I learned how to lie.

I don't mean the small fibs that children tell. I mean real lies fed by real fears—things I said and did that took me out of the life I'd always known and put me down hard into a new one.

It was the autumn of 1943 when my steady life began to spin, not only because of the war that had drawn the whole world into a screaming brawl, but also because of the dark-hearted girl who came to our hills and changed everything.

At times, I was so confused that I felt like the stem of a pinwheel surrounded by whir and clatter, but through that whole unsettling time I knew that it simply would not do to hide in the barn with a book and an apple and let events plunge forward without me. It would not do to turn twelve without earning my keep, and by that I meant my place, my small authority, the possibility that I would amount to something.

But there was more to it than that.

The year I turned twelve, I learned that what I said and what I did mattered.

So much, sometimes, that I wasn't sure I wanted such a burden.

But I took it anyway, and I carried it as best I could.

CHAPTER ONE

It began with the china piggy bank that my aunt Lily had given me for my fifth Christmas.

My mother was the one who noticed when it went missing.

"Are you hiding your piggy bank, Annabelle?" She was scrubbing down the baseboards in my bedroom while I put away my summer clothes. She must have noticed that the bank was missing because there was little else in my small room beyond the furniture itself and the windows, a comb and a brush and a book beside my bed. "Nobody's going to take your things," she said. "You don't need to hide them." She was on her hands and knees, her whole body wagging as she scrubbed, the soles of her black work shoes turned up for a change.

I was glad she couldn't see my face. I was folding a too-pink church dress that I hoped to outgrow by next spring, and I imagined that my face was turning the same awful color.

When I'd come home from school that day, I had shaken the china pig to get out a penny and had dropped it by mistake, breaking it into bits and spilling out the coins that I'd been saving for years and which must have added up to nearly ten dollars by now. I had buried the pieces of broken china beyond the kitchen garden and gathered the coins in an old hankie, tied up the corners, and hidden the bundle in a winter boot under my bed along with the silver dollar that my grandfather had given to me on my last birthday, from his collection.

I had never put that silver dollar in my bank because I didn't think of it as money. It was like a medal that I imagined wearing someday, so beautiful was the woman on it, so splendid and serious in her spiky crown.

And I determined that I would part with a penny, maybe even more, but I would not give up that silver dollar to the terrible girl waiting on the path that led into Wolf Hollow.

Every day, to get to school, I walked with my brothers—Henry, who was nine, and James, who was seven—down into Wolf Hollow and then back up out of it again to return home. And that was where a big, tough, older girl named Betty had said she'd be waiting for me after school.

She had been sent from the city to stay with her grandparents, the Glengarrys, who lived above the bank of Raccoon Creek, just past the end of the lane to our farm. I'd been afraid of her since the day she appeared at the schoolhouse three weeks earlier.

It was whispered that Betty had been sent to the country because she was *incorrigible*, a word I had to look up in the big dictionary at the schoolhouse. I didn't know if living in the country with her grandparents was meant to be a punishment or a cure, but either way I didn't think it was fair to inflict her on us who had not done anything so terribly wrong.

She arrived at our school one morning without any fanfare or much in the way of explanation. There were already nearly forty of us, more than the little school was meant to hold, so some had to double up at desks, two in a seat intended for one, two writing and doing sums on the slanted and deeply scarred desktop, two sets of books in the cubby under the lid.

I didn't mind so much because I shared a seat with my friend Ruth, a dark-haired, red-lipped, pale girl with a quiet voice and perfectly ironed dresses. Ruth liked to read as much as I did, so we had that one big thing in common. And we were both skinny girls who took regular baths (which wasn't true of all the students in Wolf Hollow School), so sitting tight together wasn't a bad thing.

Our teacher, Mrs. Taylor, said, "Good morning," when Betty arrived that day and stood at the back of the schoolroom. Betty didn't say anything. She crossed her arms over her chest. "Children, this is Betty Glengarry." Which sounded, to me, like a name from a song.

We were expected to say good morning, so we did. Betty looked at us without a word.

"We're a little crowded, Betty, but we'll find a seat for you. Hang up your coat and lunch pail."

We all watched in silence to see where Mrs. Taylor would put Betty, but before she had a chance to assign a seat, a thin girl named Laura, apparently reading the writing on the wall, gathered up her books and wedged in next to her friend Emily, leaving a desk free.

This became Betty's desk. It was in front of the one I shared with Ruth, close enough so that, within a couple of days, I had spitballs clinging to my hair and tiny red sores on my legs where Betty had reached back and poked me with her pencil. I wasn't happy about the situation, but I was glad that Betty had chosen to devil me instead of Ruth, who was smaller than I was and dainty. And I had brothers who had inflicted far worse upon me, while Ruth had none. For the first week after Betty arrived, I decided to weather her minor attacks, expecting them to wane over time.

In a different kind of school, the teacher might have noticed such things, but Mrs. Taylor had to trust that what was going on behind her back wasn't worth her attention.

Since she taught us all, the chairs clustered at the front of the room by the chalkboard were always occupied by whatever grade level was having a lesson while the rest of us sat at our desks and did our work until it was our turn at the front.

Some of the older boys slept through a good part of the day. When they woke up for their lessons at the chalkboard, they were so openly contemptuous of Mrs. Taylor that I believe the lessons she taught them were shorter than they might have been. They were all big boys who were useful on their farms and didn't see the point of going to a school that wouldn't teach them to sow or reap or herd anything. And they knew full well that if the war was still going on when they were old enough, school wouldn't help them fight the Germans. Being the farmers and ranchers who fed the soldiers might save them from the war, or make them strong enough to fight, but school never would.

Still, in the coldest months, the work they might be asked to do at home was tedious and difficult: mending fences and barn roofs and wagon wheels. Given the choice to spend a day snoozing and, at recess, roughhousing with the other boys instead of working in the freezing wind, the boys generally chose school. If their fathers let them.

But when Betty arrived that October, the days were still warm, and so those awful boys were not regularly attending school. If not for her, the schoolhouse would have been a peaceful place, at least until everything fell to pieces that terrible November and I was called upon to tell my catalogue of lies.

Back then, I didn't know a word that described Betty properly or what to call the thing that set her apart from the other children in that school. Before she'd been there a week, she'd taught us a dozen words we had no business knowing, poured a well of ink on Emily's sweater, and told the little kids where babies came from, something I'd only just learned from my grandmother the spring before when the calves were born. For me, learning about babies was a gentle thing that my grandmother handled with the grace and humor of someone who had borne several of her own, every one of them on the bed where she still slept with my grandfather. But for the youngest of the children at my school, it was not gentle. Betty was cruel about it. She scared them to bits. Worst of all, she told them that if they tattled to their parents, she would follow them through the woods after school and beat them, as she later did me. Maybe kill them. And they believed her, just as I did.

I could threaten my brothers with death and dismemberment a dozen times a day and they would laugh at me and stick out their tongues, but when Betty merely looked at them they settled right down. So they might not have been much help had they been with me that day in Wolf Hollow when Betty stepped out from behind a tree and stood in the path ahead of me.

When I was smaller, I asked my grandfather how Wolf Hollow got its name.

"They used to dig deep pits there, for catching wolves," he said.

He was one of the eight of us who lived together in the farmhouse that had been in our family for a hundred years, three generations tucked together under one roof after the Depression had tightened the whole country's belt and made our farm the best of all places to live. Now, with a second world war raging, lots of people grew victory gardens to help feed themselves, but our whole farm was a giant victory garden that my grandfather had spent his whole life tending.

He was a serious man who always told me the truth, which I didn't always want but sometimes asked for anyway. When I asked him how Wolf Hollow got its name, for instance, he told me, even though I was only eight at the time.

He was sitting in a chair near the stove in the kitchen, his elbows on his knees, hands hanging loose from his big wrists, pale feet ready for his boots. Different times of the year he looked like a younger man, open-eyed. That morning, even though it was only just June, he looked beat. The top of his forehead was as white as his feet, but his nose and cheeks were brown, like his hands and his arms, up to where he rolled his sleeves. I knew how weary he was, even though he spent a good part of every day sitting in the shade, doing small work.

"What did they want to catch wolves for?" You couldn't milk a wolf. Or hitch it to a plow. Or eat it for dinner, I didn't think.

"So there wouldn't be as many running around here anymore."

He wasn't looking at me. He was looking at his hands. Even though they were already tough as hide, he had a weeping blister at the base of each thumb, from helping my father with the planting.

"Eating the chickens?" I asked. Sometimes I woke up in the morning to my mother screaming at a fox that had dug its way into the henhouse. I wasn't sure even my mother would go after a wolf that way.

"Among other things." He sat up straight and rubbed his eyes. "Weren't enough people hunting wolves anymore. They were getting too brave and too many."

I thought about a pit full of wolves.

"Did they kill them after they got them in the pit?"

My grandfather sighed. "Shot 'em. Turned in their ears for the bounty. Three dollars a pair."

"Their ears? If there were pups, did they keep them for pets?"

My grandfather didn't make much noise when he laughed. It was a matter of his shoulders shaking a couple of times. "You think a wolf would get along with dogs?"

There were always plenty of dogs on the farm. I couldn't imagine the place without six or seven running around. Once in a while one would disappear, but after a time another would show up to take its place.

"But they could have raised the pups right. Made dogs out of them."

My grandfather pulled his suspenders up over his shoulders and began to put on his socks. "A wolf is not a dog and never will be," he said, "no matter how you raise it."

When he had his boots on and laced, he stood up and put one of his big hands on the top of my head. "They killed the pups, too, Annabelle. Probably didn't give it much thought. Don't forget you weren't the least bit bothered when I mashed that young copperhead last spring."

The snake had kept the imprint of his boot, like it was made of clay.

"Copperheads are poisonous," I said. "That's different."

"Not to the snake, it isn't," he'd said. "Or to the God who made it."

CHAPTER TWO

I thought about that snake as I stood on the path out of Wolf Hollow, Betty waiting ahead of me. The hair on the back of my neck rose up, and I felt a distant kinship with the wolves that had died here. Betty was wearing a gingham dress, and a blue sweater that matched her eyes, and black leather shoes. Her yellow hair was pulled back in a ponytail. On the whole, but for the expression on her face, she looked harmless.

I stopped when I was still ten feet away from her.

"Hey, Betty," I said. I held tight to the book cradled in my right arm. It was a history book that was so old it didn't even count Arizona as a state, but it had some good heft to it and I thought maybe I could throw it at her if she got too close. My lunch pail wasn't heavy enough to be much good, but I gave it a little swing with my left hand so she'd see I wasn't completely unarmed.

"What kind of a name is Annabelle?" She had a deep voice, almost boyish. She looked at me steadily, her head down like a dog's when he's thinking about whether or not to bite. She was half smiling, her arms limp at her sides. She cocked her head to one side.

I shrugged. I didn't know what kind of a name I had.

"You're the rich girl," she said. "It's a rich girl name."

I looked behind me to see if there was someone else on the path. Someone rich.

"You think I'm rich?" It had never occurred to me that I might be considered rich, although my family was an old one that had given land for the church and the school and still had enough left for a good-size farm. My ancestors lay beneath the finest headstones in the graveyard, and our house was, in fact, big enough for the three generations that now lived there, albeit cheek by jowl. We had running water. A couple of years earlier, Mr. Roosevelt had sent us the electric, and we'd had the wherewithal to wire up the house. We had a telephone mounted on our sitting room wall, which we still regarded as something of a miracle. Moreover, we did eat at Lancaster's in Sewickley maybe twice a year. But most amazing of all was the indoor privy, which my parents had recently installed, now that my grandparents were old enough to deserve it. But we were not rich.

"You got a purple window," Betty said.

I didn't know what she was talking about until I remembered the lilac glass in our front hall window, one of the things I loved best about our house. That and the gables and the slate roof that looked like silver feathers. The big fireplaces in every room. And the windows tall as doors.

"My grandma told me about your purple window," Betty said. "I never heard of a purple window before, 'cept in a church or a kingdom. Nobody has a purple window unless they's rich."

I didn't know what to say to that, so I didn't say anything.

Betty picked up a stick from along the path. It was dead wood, but I could tell from how she held it that it was still heavy.

"Tomorrow you bring me something or I'm going to beat you with this stick."

She said it so calmly that I thought she was joking, but when she took a step toward me I went hot and felt my heart thumping.

"Like what?" I said. I imagined myself lugging the purple window through the woods.

"Like whatever you have."

I didn't have much. Just my piggy bank and the coins in it and my silver dollar and my books. A beaver muff my grandfather had once made for my grandmother and which she had given to me when it got ratty. A lace collar that I snapped onto my church dresses. A pair of white cotton gloves that were too small for me now. And a sweater frog that I had borrowed from my aunt Lily and she had not asked about since.

I catalogued these assets quickly in my head, but I was not convinced that I would give Betty anything until she said, "I'll wait for your brothers if you don't come."

They were tough little boys, my brothers, but they were smaller than I was and they were mine to look after.

I didn't say anything as Betty leaned the stick against a tree and continued up the path away from me. "And don't tell nobody about it or I'll use a rock on the little one." James. She meant James. The little one.

I waited until she was out of sight and then I got my breath back and thought about what it would feel like to be hit with a stick.

A year earlier Henry had thrown a toadstool the size of a dinner plate at me and I'd stepped back out of the way and tripped over a dog and broken my arm. I'd burned myself a couple of times, stepped on a hoe blade and snapped the handle back into my forehead, sprained my ankle in a groundhog hole. Nothing much else had done me bodily

16

harm in my eleven years on earth, but I'd been hurt enough to know that a whack with a branch wouldn't kill me.

Still, as I passed it, I heaved the particular stick she had chosen as far as I could into the woods. There were plenty of other sticks around, but I felt a little better as I cast this one beyond her reach.

I decided, as I plodded slowly up the path, that Betty wouldn't go after Henry or James until she tried me, so I'd wait to see if she was a barker or a biter before telling my parents anything that might make Betty a whole lot angrier than she already was. But I confessed to myself that I was afraid in a way I hadn't known before.

I hadn't felt very much true fear in my life, except about the war . . . that it might still be raging when my brothers grew old enough to fight the Nazis . . . even though farm boys were often spared. Even though by that time someone would surely have won. And I was afraid of that, too—who would win, who would lose.

We girls in the 4-H club had made a flag to hang in the church, adding a blue star every time someone from the township went off to fight. When one of them died, we changed the blue star to a gold one. Just two, so far, but I had been to their funerals, and I knew that there was no "just" about it.

I sometimes sat with the grown-ups and listened to the

radio in the evenings after the supper dishes were done. Nobody said anything when the news came on. My mother listened with her head bowed, her hands nested and still in her mending. The talk was of concentration camps, which I thought at first meant places where people went to think hard thoughts.

"I do wish they were that," my father said. "But they're not, Annabelle. They're prisons for people Hitler doesn't like."

I had a hard time imagining why Hitler disliked so many people.

"Who *does* he like?" I asked.

My father thought about his answer. "People with blond hair and blue eyes," he said.

Which made me glad to have hair that was brown. Eyes, too.

We listened to news of bombs and submarines, smiled at the announcement that the Allies were close to retaking Italy, worried about everything else.

"No need to be afraid, Annabelle," my mother said, running her hand down my back.

But I was.

I wasn't afraid of my mother, though, despite how hard she could sometimes be. She had forgotten what it felt like to ride a swing up into the sky, to stop hoeing at the first sign of a blister, to expect anything to be easier than it was. She had been seventeen when she'd had me, was only twenty-eight the year I learned how to lie, not much more than a girl herself, in charge of three generations and a good bit of farmwork, too. But even when she was most impatient with me, I did not fear her.

Nor was I really afraid of my aunt Lily, though she could be alarming. A tall, thin, ugly woman who might have been handsome as a man, Aunt Lily spent her days working as a postmistress and her nights praying and reading from her Bible and practicing dance steps in the small patch of floor at the foot of her bed. She sometimes invited me into her bedroom to listen to *Peter and the Wolf* on the phonograph, and now and then she put a penny into the china pig she'd given me, but her big, square teeth and her feverish devotion to God frightened me.

And there were times when I was afraid of my grand-mother's ailing heart that forced her to go up the stairs backward, sitting down . . . how weak and gray she be-came sometimes, no longer the strong and able woman she'd once been. When we could, she and I sat on the porch swing, playing I Spy, remarking on the butterflies in the front garden, hoping for a pheasant to come hopping out of the woods to poach the seed that she scattered for the songbirds. She loved those birds. Loved them. Even the drab little ones. Especially the drab little ones. There was nothing about my grandmother that frightened me, except the thought that she'd be gone soon.

But I shared that fear with everyone in our house.

Betty was mine to fear, and I decided that she was mine to disarm. If I could. On my own.

But for now I was simply happy that she was gone, and I followed so slowly that Betty was nowhere to be seen by the time I cleared the trees and made my way onto the field that was empty but for her footprints, which were deep and sharp and suggested that she was more freighted than she could possibly be.

CHAPTER THREE

Lots of people crossed our farm to get from down the hollow to the houses on the other side of our fields instead of following the road from the school all the way around the hill. I'd never minded—we knew everyone for miles around—but I was sometimes startled by the vagabonds who passed through from time to time.

In those days, not so very long after the Great Depression, there were people who had taken up wandering and didn't know how to stop—cut loose from their roots and their people—never stopping anywhere for very long. And then there were those who had come home from the first big war so shaken, so silent, that they didn't seem to know who they were any longer or where they belonged.

One of them, a man named Toby, had stayed.

He wasn't like the others.

He didn't ask for food or money. He didn't ask for anything at all. But instead of drifting through on his way to somewhere else like the others, he circled the hills endlessly, and I confess that I had been nervous about him in the beginning.

But that's before I had come to know him.

I looked for him as I walked home that day, scanning the field that wrapped itself around the long, low hill like a nubby shawl. I often saw him away in the distance as I made my way to school and home again. He liked to stand at the edge of the woods, still as a tree. Or on the very top of the hill, clear against the sky.

We didn't know where Toby had come from or much about him, except that he had been a foot soldier, fighting the Germans in France. Decades earlier. That much we'd heard, in passing, at church, at the market, and took it to be true.

His left hand, terribly scarred, seemed to confirm the story. But nobody knew for sure where he came from except that he might have stopped in these hills because they reminded him of home. Or maybe they were simply like a place where he'd always wanted to be.

A lot of people worried about Toby as he walked the woods and valleys in his long, black oilcloth coat and his black boots, long black hair and beard, and always three long guns slung across his back. They didn't know what to make of this largely silent man who never seemed to stop walking, morning to night, his head down, plodding along neither faster nor slower than he had the day before.

I sometimes pictured him huddled in a trench while a thousand Germans ran around topside with bayonets fixed and spikes on their helmets and bloodlust in their eyes. Even though I was only eleven, I knew enough about fear to conclude that being completely afraid, body and soul, was probably enough to make a person strange forever after. And that's what Toby was. Strange.

"Hard to know, but sometimes it's more than fear or shell shock that makes a man like he is," my grandmother said to me one day soon after Toby had first come to our hills. "He wouldn't have been much more than a boy when he fought in that terrible war. But he must have seen and done things that would lay a strong man low."

We'd heard that Toby was squatting in an old smoke-house in Cobb Hollow down below the Glengarry place, along where we grew potatoes and corn. Nobody owned that smokehouse anymore, not since Silas Cobb had died and his old house burned up from a lightning strike. The smokehouse was set back away from the burned-out foundation of the house, mostly hidden in the trees and brush that had grown up around it. It was a snug little place made of stone and wood with a metal roof. I'd come across it once when one of our cows went missing and we all scattered through the woods to bring her home.

I knew better than to go inside the old shacks beyond the borders of our farm, some of them built up around oil well pumps, some of them for curing meat, some for fowl, all of them apt to attract snakes. But I'd explored the old smokehouse before Toby took it for his own. Except for the smell of meat and smoke that was still strong inside, it seemed a nice enough place for a man like Toby to live. And the old well at the nearby Cobb place—though nothing more now than a hole in the earth, like the Cobb house itself—still meant water worth drinking when the nearby crick froze up.

I could imagine Toby warm inside the smokehouse, a fire in the spot where fires had once burned steadily. Perhaps he used the meat hooks dangling from the rafters overhead to hang his coat when he wasn't in it, his guns when they weren't slung across his back. On one, his black hat. On another, his camera.

We'd all been surprised when Toby had asked to borrow our camera, which was now his, more or less. It was amazing that he had spoken at all, that he had come close enough to any of us to make such a request, that he had suddenly seemed excited about something, especially something like photographs. But he had, and the whole thing had been an accident.

When I was seven and Henry five, James three, my mother had taken us to Horne's, the big department store in Pittsburgh, to have our portrait done. My mother had one picture of herself, taken with her whole family shortly before her mother died. It was pressed in the family Bible, brown as summer dust. My father had many portraits of his forebears, a furious bunch of Scots: beetle-browed, mash-mouthed, goat-eyed. But nowhere in our house was there a simple picture of any of us smiling, arm in arm. My mother wanted such a thing, of her children, so she took the three of us to Horne's and had us sit together for our portrait. The photographer told her that all portraits taken that month would be entered into a contest for a Kodak camera and a lifetime supply of film and processing.

"And when would I have time to take pictures of anything?" she said, smiling, as she paid the man.

Three weeks later, when a package arrived for my mother, we were astonished to find that it contained both our portrait, in which we all looked sweeter than we really were, and the news that we had won the camera. It was also enclosed, along with a dozen spools of film to get us started and some special envelopes for sending them in to be developed.

It was as if we had received a tiny spaceship or a time machine, so astounding was this gift.

Word soon spread, and before long our neighbors were dropping in on Sunday afternoons, still in their church clothes, angling for pictures. My mother was too busy to oblige them. Aunt Lily was willing to take the pictures, but she was so bossy and critical of her subjects that they always looked as if they'd had the flu in their pictures. When people saw the results, they asked for another round with another photographer, which was a waste of film and time. I tried my hand at it, but I tended to lop off their heads.

So people stopped coming after a while and the camera gathered dust until one afternoon—when the peaches were in their brief blossom and the sun behind them made a rosy miasma of the orchard—I took the camera out to try to save the sight.

I stood at the top of the orchard and took one picture after another, lowering the camera in between to sigh and breathe the chill, pink air.

At some point I became aware of Toby standing off to one side near the outermost trees, watching me.

I'd never spoken to him, had always found myself at least a field away from him until now. And I'd never known him to watch a person the way he was watching me. To stand still for so long in one place.

I slowly pointed the camera in his direction, expecting him to shy from it as if it were a gun, but he didn't. I took his picture, even though—through the lens, from such a distance—he looked like nothing but a smudge of darkness in a hat.

When he began to walk toward me I waited. It was full light out and I was on my own farm. There was no reason to be nervous. That's what I told myself. But I was only nine back then, too young to be very brave. Toby was a tall man who never smiled. Seldom spoke. Had those terrible scars on his hand. And those guns.

I could hear someone hammering something in the distance, probably my father fixing siding on the barn. The sound kept me where I was as Toby walked up to me. When he was a dozen feet away I became aware of the smoke-and-meat smell coming off him, mixed with his own scent. It wasn't entirely unpleasant, but it was overlaid with the stink of kerosene from his lamp. Whenever the dogs got near him, they'd shake their heads and sneeze.

He looked at the camera and then at me. "Is that yours?" he said.

"My mother's." I thought about it. "And mine." It was, after all, my picture that had won the camera. Mine and James's and Henry's.

Toby hitched his gun belt higher on his shoulder. I'd

held a gun before. Three must have been very heavy. His black coat, long and stiff, had a high collar that framed his neck and made him look bigger than he was. Like some animals will ruff up their fur for purposes of warfare.

"You taking pictures of the blossoms?"

I nodded. "And you. Just one of you. Do you want it when it comes in?"

Toby shook his head. "I know what I look like."

I wondered how many years it had been since he'd seen himself in a mirror.

He was staring at the camera. I took the strap from around my neck. "You want to try?" I held the camera out toward him.

Toby glanced at me and then away. At me again. And away. At the blossoms, then back over his shoulder toward the fields just plowed for planting. At a line of blue spruce higher than anything else for a mile. He walked close, took the camera, stepped back.

"I'll bring it back tomorrow, if that's all right."

I was a little startled. From saying nothing to me, ever, to now taking this liberty was surprising. But I didn't know how to say no, not to an adult, and I didn't think my mother would mind. She often made an extra loaf of bread or pot of jam for Toby. She wasn't scared of him. I didn't think she'd mind if he used the camera for a day.

And so that was the beginning of a change in our lives. Had we not won the Kodak, had the peach blossoms been less beautiful that year, had Toby been elsewhere on his walk that day, had I fled from the sight of him, had I said no, Toby would not have learned how to take the pictures he took and, eventually, been given the camera for his own. Nor would I have come to know him as I did; and he, me.

We would have been spared some trouble if we had not crossed paths that day. But it's important to look at how everything ended and not just what happened along the way.

CHAPTER FOUR

My mother gave me a funny look as I stood at the back door the next morning, readying myself, before setting off for school. When she said, "Something wrong, Annabelle?" I nearly told her about Betty. It would have been a relief to put the whole thing in her hands.

But although there were only apples and potatoes, beets and a few winter squash left to bring in, and although she, of all women on earth, was capable and strong, I had it in mind to spare her this particular battle. I'd thought it through: If I told her, she'd have to go to her friends, the Glengarrys, and tell them that their granddaughter was a hooligan, something they surely already knew but would not want to hear from a neighbor.

And despite the fact that she'd been able to fix nearly

every broken thing in our lives, my mother could not promise me that Betty would not come at me again, even angrier—or, worse, go after my brothers—if I tattled on her.

I had learned what *incorrigible* meant. A scolding was not going to change anything, and so far Betty hadn't done anything to deserve more.

So I said, "Nothing, Mother," and went on out the door to school, the penny from my piggy bank like an anvil in my pocket.

Henry and James were waiting in the yard for me, which made no sense at all since they took off at a run as soon as they saw me coming. Before we were even out of sight of the house, they had run well up the lane, flinging lumps of dirt at each other and stirring up a tail of dust as if they were small, unbottled genies.

Up the lane and across the spent field at the top of the hill I walked alone—all the crops here plowed under—watching for arrowheads on the crests of the furrows.

Sometimes, from this hilltop, I would be surprised by a deer. One minute, the fields below me would seem empty. The next—there, a deer—nearly invisible against the plowed dirt.

So it was with Toby that morning. One minute, the crest of the hill to my right was empty. The next, there he was, standing in the distance, still, looking toward me.

It gave me a start to see him.

I waved good morning.

I was not put out when he did not wave back. It meant nothing at all except that he wasn't like other people. Toby wasn't friendly, but he had been good to me when he didn't have to be.

Like the time I was skirting the edge of a newly planted field and stepped in a groundhog hole, spraining my ankle so badly that I couldn't walk on it. I was alone. There was no one else around. Still, I called out a couple of times as I tried to limp along. And Toby came.

I was younger then and didn't weigh all that much, but it couldn't have been easy to carry me up over the hill and down the lane to my mother, baby-style.

Close to him like that, I was most aware of his own scent and not the smokehouse's where he lived. He smelled a lot like the woods in thaw or a dog that's been out in the rain. Strong, but not really dirty.

Along the way I said a number of things: *Thank you. I'm sorry. You're nice to help me like this.* And then, at the door to the mudroom, *Will you come in for a drink of water?*

He replied to none of it, though his silence didn't feel mean.

He did not come in for a drink. In fact, he left me on the step and then strode off, back up the lane, and was gone before my mother came to the door to find that I was the one knocking.

Another time, when my father hurt his back and was laid up for a couple of days in the middle of pumpkin harvest, my mother and grandpap and we small kids arrived at the patch one morning prepared to do the work without him, only to find that the flatbed we'd left empty the night before was now loaded with pumpkins, ready for market.

No one else took credit for this kindness, and I knew that it was Toby's.

I pictured him in the darkness, working by moonlight and night-eyes, lugging the pumpkins to the wagon, some of them bigger than one man should have been able to carry. It must have taken him all night.

My mother baked a pumpkin pie for him that very day and gave it to me to take to the top of the lane in the hope of seeing him nearby. The pie was still warm in my hands. I waited long enough that the pie had cooled before I left it in a crate where we sometimes put food and hand-me-downs for Toby when he wasn't around.

Two days later, I found that he'd left the clean pie plate in the crate along with a posy of bittersweet and wild asters tied with a leaf of quack grass.

I headed down the slope and took the path into the woods, not at all watchful. The boys had scared away any bear within earshot, snakes were somewhere sunny and warm, and I did not expect to see Betty until after school. But suddenly there she was, just as before, standing in the path ahead of me.

The stick in her hand was smaller than the first, which worried me. She'd chosen yesterday's to make an impression. Today's was a better size for swinging. And green, which meant hard. And I admit that I was afraid.

"Hey, Betty," I said as I made to walk right on by her.

She stepped in front of me and put out a hand. "We'll walk to school together," Betty said. "First you give me what you brung."

I was tempted to correct her poor English, but I didn't. I was tempted to try to push past her, but I was pretty sure that wouldn't work.

"We're not rich," I said, as if to get at least that one thing straight. "I ain't got anything to give you." The "ain't got" hurt and surprised me on its way out; some part of my brain had assumed that stooping a little might actually make me stronger, but in the next instant I could see that it hadn't.

Before I had time to think about moving, Betty had swung the stick in a small, tight arc. She'd chosen my hip, perhaps because a bruise there would not show. I worked hard not to let her see how much it hurt.

"Give me what you brung," she said.

I hated to give her anything at all. Even the penny in my pocket.

"This is the only thing I'm going to give you," I said, holding the penny out on a tight palm, the way I knew to feed a dog. "Don't ask me for anything more. I don't have anything else."

Betty looked at the penny, picked it up with her finger-tips, peered into my face. "A penny?"

"You can get two pieces of hard candy for that," I said.

"I don't want two pieces of hard candy," she said. She tossed the penny into the undergrowth. "Tomorrow you bring me something better than a penny."

"I don't have anything else to bring you, Betty. And I think it's just mean of you to be like this. We could be friends, you know," I said, quite aware that I sounded pretty dubious as I said it. "If you would stop being so mean."

Betty's answer was to swing the stick again. Harder this time—hitting the same spot, which was already aching—and I was on my knees before I knew it. When I looked up, Betty was staring at me, her face slack, her mouth hanging open a little.

She made me think of the strays that wandered onto

the farm now and again but were not taken up by our pack.

I saw her fingers tighten on the stick and I knew she was going to hit me again, and the tears came.

Her fingers relaxed on the stick. Her eyes cleared. "You're just a dumb baby," she said. "Remember what I said before. If you tell anyone, that little boy will pay for it. Now git."

I gathered myself up and let the hill take me down toward school.

At a curve in the path, I glanced back. Betty was bent low in the place where she'd thrown my penny, folding back the undergrowth with her open hands.

When I went to Aunt Lily's room that evening, she was brushing her hair. She did that a lot. And put on lipstick, then wiped it off.

"What do you want, Annabelle?" She looked at me in her mirror.

"Well." I held my hands behind my back. "I wondered if I could borrow your sweater frog again," I said, though I knew it was still up in my room. "The one with the glittery stones on it." One stone was missing, which was probably why Aunt Lily had lent it to me in the first place. It was old and a little bent, too. Not worth anything.

"My sweater frog?" With a fingertip, she stirred the dish of notions she kept on her dresser. "But you already have it, Annabelle. I haven't seen it since I lent it to you, have I?"

The little question she tacked onto the end gave me some hope.

"Haven't you?" I said, which wasn't a lie. How could a question be a lie?

"No. I don't believe I have. And I don't remember you returning it." Aunt Lily turned on her stool and looked at me from across the room. "But if I don't have it, I can't very well lend it to you again, can I? Go see if it's still up in your room somewhere." She turned back to the mirror, a pair of tweezers in her hand.

As I turned to leave, she said, "All your sweaters have buttons on them, Annabelle. No reason on earth to bother with a frog."

I shrugged. All of her sweaters had buttons, too. "It's just pretty," I said.

"Pretty. Nothing less important in the eyes of God, Annabelle, than pretty."

It was a good supper we had that night: chops fried in bacon fat, potatoes baked soft, and slaw my mother made with cream and sweet onions.

After supper, when we were clearing everything away, my mother wrapped two rolls, a chop, and an apple in a scrap of oilcloth and tied it up by its corners. "Take this up the lane," she said. "If you don't see Toby, leave it in his box. But make sure you close the lid tight or the dogs will get into it."

There were times when my mother told Toby he was "entirely too thin" or that he needed "some color" and she'd send me with something extra for him to eat. She didn't dare send my brothers, who would use the excuse to horse around out in the dark until there was no time left for homework, barely enough for a bath.

"Squirrel is not enough for a grown man," she said as she handed me the bundle.

"There's plenty of culls in the orchard," I said, "and potatoes and beets not too far from his shack. I don't know why he's so thin."

My mother just looked at me. "Do you think he would take something without our say-so?" She shook her head. "Well, he would not."

I considered her answer. "Then why don't we say so?"

"Never mind that," she said, turning again to the sink. "Just get going and back again before it's too dark to see where you're putting your feet."

"And why doesn't he just ask?" I said, though my mother's back usually meant she'd said all she had to say.

"Same as I said before," she said without turning. "Now go on before all the light's gone."

CHAPTER FIVE

Toby appeared in layers as I walked up the steep lane: first his hatted head, then more and more of him down to his boots as I reached the flat ground at the top of the lane. He was a scarecrow, but for the guns on his back and his arms hanging loose at his sides.

If he saw me coming, he made no sign of it. Toby never came to meet a person.

"Hey, Toby," I said. "Mother sent me with a little supper." I didn't know I would say it until I did: "We had too much for just us."

Toby's face in the shadow of his hat brim was as quiet and mild as an old dog's.

I noticed the camera hanging from his neck. "Do you have any film to send in?"

We mailed it for him when he did—gave the film to my aunt Lily, since she was the postmistress and went into the office every weekday—and I usually carried around the prints when they came back until Toby and I crossed paths. We had never once opened the package, though I was sometimes tempted. When Toby wanted us to see what he had done, he offered.

One time he had showed me a batch that featured a red-tailed hawk with a rabbit in its beak, a thunderhead glazed with evening light, a deer napping in a patch of mayapples. I had never known anyone quiet enough to approach a sleeping deer. Nor had I known any hungry man who would shoot one with a camera instead of a gun.

He took a little spool out of his pocket and handed it to me. I gave him the bundle of food.

"Do you still have some film?"

He nodded. Every time the photographs came back to us, there were two fresh rolls in the package. Kodak keeping its word.

He shifted the guns on his back a little. Didn't turn to leave right away, as he usually did.

I waited.

He reached into his pocket. "This is yours," he said, handing me a penny. It was warm when I took it.

I recalled Betty searching through the ivy along the

40

trail to school. Toby must have been watching from the trees.

I put the penny in my own pocket.

Toby waited some more, in an almost hopeful way. If he knew that it was my penny, then he had seen Betty hit me. Perhaps he had heard her threats. But he had not intervened.

If he was waiting for me to tell him about it, to ask for his help, I couldn't. I just wasn't sure how I felt about all that.

With a last little nod, Toby turned and walked away, his guns and boots making their simple music. How he stilled it at will was beyond me. I had never yet been able to surprise so much as a milk cow, let alone a doe.

I stayed for a bit and watched him make his way back across the turned ground between the strawberry patch and the woods, dipping and rising a little as he walked against the grain of the furrows, like a boat crossing a small sea.

On my way back down the lane I paused at the sight of my house in the growing darkness, lit from within, and wondered if Toby ever stood where I did, saw what I saw.

Fingering the penny in my pocket, I thought that perhaps he did.

I found my father sitting on the back step. He always seemed to be there when I returned from taking Toby some supper. "And how was Toby tonight?" he asked as he followed me into the house.

"Same as ever," I said. "Quiet."

"I do like that about him," my father said. "But you should tell me if he ever worries you, Annabelle."

Which startled me. "Like how?" I said.

My father shrugged. "Anything at all."

"Like if he seems sick or if he's hurt, you mean?"

He answered by putting his hand on the top of my head and smiling a little.

"Go on and do your homework now," he said.

But first I went in search of my aunt Lily, who would send in the film that Toby had given me, neither of us knowing that, on that small spool, another piece of trouble was waiting for someone to find it.

As I got ready for bed that night, I examined my aching hip and the bruise that Betty had given me. It looked like a red cucumber, not yet gone to black, sore to the touch.

And I made up my mind right then that she would not have Aunt Lily's sweater frog. It wasn't possible that even a girl like Betty would hurt my brothers, or me, beyond a bruise shaped like a cucumber. That sort of thing didn't happen. And knowing that Toby might be nearby gave me some reassurance. I was certain that he wouldn't let anything really bad happen to me or my brothers. If he was nearby at the time. If he saw it happening.

And if I did get another bruise in the bargain, I would tell my mother. She would know what to do.

When my brothers ran off ahead of me the next morning, I ran too and kept them close to me—and me close to them—up the lane and down the other side of the hill, across the fields, toward Wolf Hollow. More than once they stopped to look at me, and at one point Henry said, "You're fast for a girl," and another time James told me to slow down and get lost. "We can walk to school by our own selves," he yelled as he put on speed.

Which was true, of course, but beside the point.

When we reached the path into Wolf Hollow, I caught up with them and grabbed James by the arm. "I want to walk with you the rest of the way," I said.

James shook me off with an uh-uh, but Henry said, "What's wrong?"

"Nothing," I said. "Except I saw a big snake on the path yesterday."

Henry seemed to accept this. He knew how I felt about snakes.

James, big-eyed: "A king snake?"

I nodded. "Biggest one I've ever seen."

"Well, nuts, Annabelle. I would have come back for a look if you'd told us yesterday."

"Which is why I didn't tell you yesterday," I said. "But let's go quietly and maybe we'll see him again."

So it was that the three of us were together on the path when Betty stepped out from behind a tree.

The boys stopped so suddenly that I bumped into them. "Hey, Betty," Henry said. James just stood still. I cut around in front of the boys and continued down the path.

"Come on," I said, "or we'll be late for school."

I didn't look back. The boys followed close by. At the first turn in the path I ushered them ahead and off they ran, and so did I, all the way down the hill and into the schoolhouse.

"I don't like that Betty," James said as we unbuttoned our jackets and hung up our caps. "She's spooky."

"She's just a dumb girl," Henry said, but he kept his voice down and looked over his shoulder when he said it.

Betty arrived then, but she paid us no attention at all.

She focused, instead, on her desk. In it sat one of the biggest boys, Andy Woodberry. I liked that name—Woodberry—but I didn't like Andy. Nobody did. Not even the other big boys, though they did whatever he told them to do.

Andy had not been in school since before Betty joined us. He and his father and uncles worked side-by-side farms not too far from ours: dairy cows, mostly, but corn, too, and hay and potatoes. A kitchen garden. Enough ewes for wool and Sunday dinner lamb in the spring. Chickens. Some goats. Pretty much what you'd expect at a dairy.

End of October, Andy came to school from time to time, mostly for a change of scenery, I thought. He paid no attention to his lessons or to Mrs. Taylor.

"You're in my seat," Betty said to him. Even sitting down, he was nearly as tall as she was, standing, but she didn't seem the least bit nervous.

The other children had gone quiet, watching. Mrs. Taylor, writing a lesson on the chalkboard, hadn't yet noticed.

Andy looked Betty up and down. "Who are you?" he said.

"Betty Glengarry. Who are you?"

"Andy Woodberry."

She considered him, her hands on her hips. "Do you live in the woods?"

"No."

"Are you a berry?"

"No." He sat up straighter in his chair. "Do you live in a glen?"

"As a matter of fact, I do," she said.

Which gave him pause. "And are you a . . ." at which even Andy seemed to understand that there was no good way to finish this. Betty was already smiling.

". . . a garry? No, I am not a garry. Unless a garry is a girl who means to sit at that seat you're in."

By now, Andy looked so baffled that I concluded no girl had ever spoken to him this way. Not even his ma.

If anyone had asked me, I'd have said that Betty would at the very least have burrs in her hair by the end of recess, but I would have been wrong.

Without another word, Andy stood up and waited while Betty took her seat. Then he stood looming over Benjamin, the small boy in the desk next to hers, until he gathered up his things with a sigh and shoved in next to someone else.

Andy sat down and stretched out his legs. His pant cuffs and boot laces bristled with sticktights.

When Mrs. Taylor turned from the chalkboard and saw him sitting there, her shoulders went up and down slowly, and she slumped a little.

"Good morning, Mr. Woodberry," she said. "Have you brought your books with you?"

"Don't need books," he said, tapping his head. "Got it all up here."

I was sitting behind Betty, but when she turned toward Andy I could see that she was smiling. "He can share with me, Mrs. Taylor," Betty said. "I don't mind."

"Well, that's very nice of you," said Mrs. Taylor.

"It sure is," Andy said.

From the way Betty was looking at Andy, I thought maybe she'd be inclined to pay less attention to me from now on.

The rest of the morning went pretty well, though Andy fell asleep at one point and punctuated the lessons with his snoring. Betty, to wake him, laid a hand on his bare arm. When he woke, Andy gave himself a shake, yawned loudly, and crossed his arms like a lord.

He was not a bad-looking boy and was cleaner than some, but Betty was the first girl to take to him. I wondered about that: how quickly an attraction had sprung up between them. But I had seen such a thing before, when a new dog showed up on the farm. Sometimes, there was a fight before anyone knew the reason why. Sometimes, quite the reverse.

CHAPTER SIX

For the next few days, Betty seemed to ignore me. I walked to and from school without incident, spent each recess playing games with my friends, and took lessons at the chalkboard with Mrs. Taylor uneventfully, while Betty and Andy huddled at their desks behind her back, whispering and grinning. At recess, they disappeared, came back to lessons late, left school together, arrived the same way in the morning.

Everyone noticed this—what I thought of as a court-ship, odd as that seemed, given how young Betty was, just fourteen. But my own mother had married at sixteen, so I did not spend too much time questioning the thing that had made me a smaller target.

Andy's was a sporadic education at best, however, and

I soon learned that even Betty could not compete with an Indian summer day.

Walking to school that morning was pure joy. The ground was soft and fragrant, the birds talkative, and the sun somewhat hazy, as if it wore a silk stocking. Before I headed down the long slope into Wolf Hollow, I took off my jacket and hat and hung them on a peach tree that clung stubbornly to a very few leaves, and those an autumn gold.

Where my brothers were, I neither knew nor cared. I felt that with very little effort I might fly away over these hills, the sun on my back, the forest flaming gorgeously beneath me.

I might even have been whistling or singing beneath my breath as I entered the woods that morning.

I don't remember.

What came next erased most everything but the fact of Betty again.

Perhaps she had been waiting for Andy and he had not appeared, which had left her angry, with time on her hands.

Or maybe she'd simply gone too long without dominion, however small.

In any event, she was ready for me at a time when I was not ready for her.

And she had chosen a more brutal weapon than before.

Here, ahead of me on the path, was an odd sight.

Betty sat on a fallen log with something in her lap, while my brothers crouched before her, moving in an oddly slow and gentle way.

"Henry," I said.

"Shhh," he replied without turning. "She has a quail."

And she did have a quail. A hen, brown and soft. A young one from the look of her. Fresh-eyed and sleek.

Betty held her easily under her left arm. She had made a choker of her right hand, her fingers circling the bird's neck just tightly enough to hold her still. The quail blinked and murmured as the boys stroked her soft head with the tips of their small fingers.

"She's so nice," James whispered. "I wish I could have her."

"Well, maybe you can," Betty said. "Maybe you can start a quail farm."

To which Henry said, "Naw, it's a wild bird. It's not a chicken." But he said it softly, almost wistfully, and he never took his eyes off the sweet, brown darling in Betty's lap.

I stood behind them, wondering if Betty had changed but pretty sure that she hadn't.

"Come on now, boys," I said. "We're going to be late for school."

They ignored me so completely that I felt invisible.

"I'll bring her down to school with me," Betty said.

"You go on ahead. We'll be right along."

She sounded a lot like I did. Older sisterish. But they obeyed her as they never did me.

The boys backed away slowly so as not to startle the bird and then scampered off down the hill, hissing nonsense at each other as they jockeyed for the lead.

I began to follow them, but a sound drew me back.

My mother had wrung the necks of many chickens, but she had always done it so quickly that there was no time for sound or struggle.

This was different.

I turned at a rasping sound behind me. Betty held the quail out by its neck, its plump little body swinging as it fought the noose she'd made with her fingers, its talons curling and stretching, its stubby wings frantically beating the air.

"Betty!" I cried. "Let her go. You're killing her!"

I reached for the quail, and as I did Betty squeezed her hand around its neck and held it high, out of my reach, stepping back and up on the fallen log, a serious look on her face, her eyes on mine, unblinking.

"Let go!" I cried again.

But as I grabbed for the bird, she squeezed her fist all the way shut, crushing its neck. I heard the sound of the delicate bones snapping.

She tossed the poor, limp thing at me, and I backed away, tripping on a root in the path and landing hard on my back.

Where Toby came from, I don't know. One minute, I was lying on the path, struggling to regain my wits, and the next he was between us, his back to me, snarling like a farm dog.

I don't know what he did. I couldn't see Betty at all. Just Toby. And I couldn't make out a word of what he said to her. Mostly it was noise. Terrible noise.

And then he turned and helped me to my feet without uttering another sound. He gathered up the dead bird. She looked small and perfect in his ruined hand.

He took a breath and straightened himself before heading up the path and out of Wolf Hollow.

All of it, from my brothers running off, to Toby leaving us, had taken less than a minute.

Betty lay on her back in the undergrowth, wide-eyed and almost smiling.

"What did you do that for?" I said, as amazed as I'd ever been. "What's the matter with you?"

"He stole my bird," she said, almost to herself. "And he said he'd make me sorry if I touched you again."

How it was possible to be pleased under the circumstances was a mystery to me, but I was. Just a little.

Perhaps Betty had met her match in Toby.

"What a dumb nut," she said, gaining her feet. She brushed herself off. Leaves stuck to her hair.

She clearly didn't realize that she'd been lying in a bed of poison ivy, and I wasn't about to tell her.

If I went to hell for wishing a plague upon her, then that's where I would go.

"You're nothing but bad," I said to her. "Right to your bones."

Which made her laugh. "My grandma taught me to wring a chicken's neck and we ate it all up that very night, with mashed potatoes and gravy. Nothing bad about it. And if there was, then she's bad, too, and your own mother with her."

I shook my head. "That's not the same thing and you know it," I said, though I wondered if she did.

I left her there, musing in that patch of poison, and prayed that she would wake tomorrow with scarlet boils and hard scabs. I prayed for a rash to veil her face with pustules and scales. And I prayed for scars. I did. I prayed for scars on the hands that had killed that harmless bird. And I wasn't sorry that I did.

By afternoon recess, Betty was scratching her neck. By the time school let out, a rash had broken out across one cheek.

And when I got home that day, I found my mother down below the house in a bed of jewelweed that grew where a spring welled from the ground.

"What are you doing?" I called to her from the lane.

She waved for me to join her, so I followed the path past the kitchen garden to where the spring had birthed a little downhill stream.

Had there been a frost hard enough to freeze the jewelweed, there would have been nothing but muck around the spring, but most of it was still green and living, if leggy. The translucent seedpods that had grown from its orange blossoms had long since burst, scattering their cargo, but enough of the leaves remained.

My mother had pulled a number of the watery stems, folding them up into a peck basket, and began to pile more into my arms.

"We're going to need a lot of this," she said. "Betty Glengarry managed to wander into a patch of poison ivy and she's covered with blisters." My mother shook her head. "I thought everyone knew better, but apparently Betty's never had poison ivy before. She'll know better now."

A baby ant wandered from a leaf and onto my hand. I blew it off. "Why do you have to do all this?" I said. "They don't have any jewelweed by their own spring?"

My mother stopped to give me a look. "Mr. Glengarry

went to Ohio to help his sister move house, and Mrs. Glengarry has sciatica. She isn't about to go traipsing around the woods when we have plenty right here." She pulled out another fistful of weeds and stuffed them into my arms. "She called to see if we had any still growing so late. And we do. So I'm going to make some broth. And you're going to help me."

I wanted to tell her about the quail, but I didn't want to talk about it. I felt sick when I remembered the sound those bones had made as they broke. And I needed time to think about the rest of it, too, and what to do next.

I thought about the quail. I thought about my brothers. I remembered the sound that Toby had made in his fury.

"All right," my mother said. "That should be more than enough for one girl."

She picked up her basket and led the way back up the hill to the house.

Together, we began a brew to soothe the hurt I'd prayed for.

In our biggest pot, we boiled water and stuffed the jewelweed in, one stalk at a time. In moments, the stems and soft leaves melted down and greened the water, filling the kitchen with a smell much like spinach makes as it cooks.

"Who's been into the ivy poison?" my grandmother called from the back room where she was catnapping.

"Betty Glengarry," my mother called. "She's got it terrible."

"City girl," my grandmother said, but not unkindly. "She'll know better next time."

Despite my better self, I hoped there *would* be a next time and that it would come after a good, hard frost.

When we'd boiled up all the weeds, we poured the broth into Mason jars, let it cool, fitted the jars with lids, and tucked them back into the peck basket.

"This ought to do the trick," my mother said. "Get your coat on. We'll take this over there and pull some beets on our way back."

"Do I have to go?" I asked. "I can start supper while you're gone."

"We won't be long," my mother said, lugging the basket into the mudroom. "Now go run out to the barn and fetch your grandpap. It's too far to walk with all this heavy business."

I vowed to stay in the truck with my grandfather while my mother made her delivery. But when we pulled up in front of the Glengarrys' house, she put a jar in each of my hands and hustled me ahead of her. "You helped make the medicine," she said. "Betty should know that. Maybe you two can be friends."

There was nothing I could say to that, so I said nothing.

When Mrs. Glengarry answered our knock she looked uncommonly upset. "Good grief, Sarah, come in. Come in,

Annabelle. You are angels. Nothing less. Wait until you see Betty. Goodness, but she's awfully sick."

And she was. "Good grief" didn't approach what I wanted to say when I saw her. Blisters I had prayed for. And blisters I had got.

Wherever Betty's skin had touched the poison ivy, she was ferociously red and swollen, some of the blisters so huge that I could see through the skin to where the fluid had collected inside. I was reminded of a bullfrog in full croak, its throat bulging out in a bubble.

It was difficult to look at her. It was more difficult to look away. I'd never seen anyone poisoned the way Betty was.

"Lord, that's quite a case you've got there," my mother said, taking off her coat and laying it on the foot of Betty's bed. "Margaret, get some clean rags, will you?"

While Betty's grandmother fetched the rags, my mother gently moved Betty's arms and legs out from her body and tucked her hair away from her face. "You poor thing," my mother said. "You must itch terribly."

Betty watched my mother as she worked. Through her teeth, she said, "I don't care." She wheezed a little. "It's just a stupid rash."

My mother shook her head. "What a brave girl you are, Betty."

"Rags," Mrs. Glengarry said, piling them on the foot of the bed. "What else?"

"Get a basin. Annabelle, bring me two of those jars."

One of God's best ideas was to invent jewelweed. As miracles went, it didn't quite stack up to parting the seas or turning water into wine, but if anything could make Betty well, it could.

My mother poured the warm broth into the basin, soaked the rags in it, squeezed them out until they were just weeping, and laid them on Betty's horrible skin until nothing showed but her eyes, which followed me as I looked around her bedroom.

Her room was a lot like mine. A bed. A small table with a lamp on it. A chair in one corner. A closet, its door open enough so I could see that there wasn't much inside. Plain white walls. A bare wood floor. A picture of Jesus on one wall. On another, a photograph of a man and a woman in good clothes, he wearing a tie, she a red hat.

Standing here in her room, with Betty laid out on the bed, helpless, and two grown-ups close by, I gave my curiosity a little rein. "Are those your parents, Betty?" I asked.

But it was Mrs. Glengarry who answered me. "Yes, that's my son, Betty's father, though he's . . ." She pulled up short. Looked around at my mother.

"Gone," Betty said, the same way she might have said *mud*.

I didn't know what *gone* meant.

"There now," my mother said. She pulled a blanket up to Betty's chin and cleared off the bed.

Betty turned her head slightly, caught me looking at her, and turned away again, but not before I had seen her eyes. They were a sore kind of red. The rags draped across her face dripped jewelweed brew into her hair. And maybe something more.

Despite all her meanness, I was glad, suddenly, that in this mild November there had still been jewelweed for us to gather.

"Do that every hour," my mother told Mrs. Glengarry, handing her the basin. "Don't wring the rags out too dry. They need to be good and wet. And don't let her get chilled."

At the door, my mother stopped and said quietly, "Margaret, if that wheezing gets any worse, give her some of the broth to drink and call Doctor Benson."

"I will, Sarah. Thank you. Thank you. And you, too, Annabelle. Betty always says such nice things about you. Maybe you could come over and play when she's well."

It was dark when we reached the beet field, but we worked by the truck's headlamps and had enough beets for supper in no time at all.

I would have gladly stayed in the field longer, doing

such work, satisfied with the fat surprise that dangled from each cluster of greens I pulled.

They didn't look like much, those beets. Tough skins clotted with dirt, hairy with fine roots, hard as stones. But inside were sweet rubies, eager to be warmed into softness.

I longed for that order of things.

CHAPTER SEVEN

The jewelweed worked, but not as quickly as it might have on a milder case, so I was happy with the day that followed. Betty stayed at home, recovering. And Andy was still fair-weathering somewhere else. Mrs. Taylor opened the windows of the schoolhouse to let in the breeze and the sound of birds. And I learned about a thing called onomatopoeia, which I could not yet spell but practiced under my breath throughout the afternoon.

The next morning, Betty and Andy both returned to school.

Betty's face and hands still looked tender, a little scalded, but so much improved that I could hardly believe she'd been so recently poisoned. Even so, she wore long sleeves and trousers and moved a little carefully as she came down the path and into the schoolyard.

I watched her from the schoolhouse steps where I sat in the sunshine with Ruth and some of the other girls, waiting for Mrs. Taylor to call us in.

"Hey, Betty," someone said.

Betty stopped, then came closer, her lunch pail in her left hand. She looked straight at me, lifted her right hand, and squeezed it slowly into a fist.

"Hey, Annabelle," she said with a smile.

I hadn't expected any thanks for helping her get well. But I hadn't expected this either. How stupid I was.

"Why are you so mean?" I asked. And I was really curious. I really wanted to know.

"I'm just older than you, is all," she said. "You'll learn to look after your own self, too. If you're not too dumb, which you might well be."

But I wasn't. Neither dumb nor too young to know what mean was.

"Come on inside," Mrs. Taylor called.

Only Betty stayed behind when the rest of us went in.

When she did eventually appear, nearly an hour later, Andy was with her.

He was newly brown with sun, his clothes clean. And Betty, despite her trousers, looked all girl next to him.

"I'm so glad you could finally join us," Mrs. Taylor said to Andy. "I hope you're feeling better," she said to Betty.

They took their seats, the lesson at the chalkboard resumed, and the rest of the morning passed quietly enough.

Andy slept through a good deal of it. As he slept, Betty watched him, ignoring Mrs. Taylor's instructions, the book on her desk closed. When he woke, Betty smiled and tugged on his sleeve. He turned to her, grinned through a yawn, and sat up straighter in his chair.

I thought about asking Mrs. Taylor if I could switch seats with someone so I wouldn't have to watch such moonshine. But I didn't want to abandon Ruth, and I seemed to be invisible to Betty as long as Andy was nearby. I didn't want to do anything to change that.

I wanted nothing more of bruises and threats and poor dead quails.

I wanted nothing to do with anyone who could close her hand around a bird's neck and smile about it.

I wanted Betty to go back where she'd come from.

I wanted to rewind the clock to where it had been before she arrived. I wanted to undo. To unremember. To be who I'd been before: someone who had never prayed for blisters. Someone who had never even considered doing so.

But if all I could have was a little respite from her

attention, I would take it, and gladly. Andy drew her to him, away from me, and I would have to be satisfied with that.

Recess, for us, was a matter of spilling out into the clearing around the schoolhouse twice each day to jump rope or play hopscotch or otherwise sow some oats. We weren't supposed to go near the road that led past the schoolhouse, through the hollow where one hill ended and another began. And we generally ignored the cars that traveled past from time to time, but whenever I heard a team of horses plodding by, pulling a hay wagon or a flatbed, I'd stop what I was doing to walk alongside for a bit, chatting with the farmers or the horses, sometimes taking them a bucket of well water if they stopped to rest on a hot afternoon.

On this day, Mr. Faas and his grays came slowly down the road pulling a wagon full of fat apples in bushels and pecks, on his way to market.

Mr. Faas was so friendly and kind that he always asked us to call him Mr. Ansel, which we did, though when Henry once called him Ansel without the "mister" my mother cuffed him behind the ear.

"Hi, Mr. Ansel," I called from the steps of the schoolhouse where Ruth and I were playing a game of cat's cradle. At which Mr. Ansel slowed the horses further and waved in reply. His "good morning" came out "goot morgan," his tongue forever German no matter how many years he'd lived in these hills.

"And how are you, small Annabelle, smaller Ruth, on a morning as fine as this one?" He wore overalls that were Sunday-clean and crisply pressed, a well-brushed hat and boots as polished as his apples, which gleamed in the sun as if he were carting them to a jeweler's for setting.

"Just fine," I said. His horses stamped a little, eager to get going, but I leaned my forehead for a moment against the nearest haunch and patted it with my open hands. "I just wish I were going to market with you and these sweet boys. They're awfully nice."

Ruth—her dark hair in a tight braid, her skirt straight and sharp—kept back a little, clear of their hooves and their big yellow teeth. Her father was a bookkeeper. The only animal at Ruth's house was a tabby cat.

Later, everyone would wonder what Ruth had ever done to deserve what happened next.

The rock that caught Ruth square in the eye was small enough so her brow did not deflect it, large enough that it knocked her on her back and did her eye real hurt. That much was clear even to me as I watched the blood spill down her cheek.

Ruth was stunned the way a bird is stunned when it

flies into a window full of sky reflected. She lay still, but her hands and feet twitched in the dust kicked up by her fall.

I knew when Mr. Ansel leaped from the wagon seat and knelt next to Ruth.

I knew when there was yelling and confusion in the schoolyard.

I knew when Mrs. Taylor came racing into the road, saw Ruth's face, and sped away again to fetch her car.

I knew when Ruth came out of her stupor and began to scream. When Mr. Ansel scooped Ruth up and into the back of Mrs. Taylor's Ford, and we both stood clear as she pulled into the road and away, quickly, dust rising in her wake.

"I will go as quickly as I can and tell her parents," Mr. Ansel said to me.

There was a smear of blood on his perfectly clean coat.

He climbed into the wagon and snapped the reins smartly. His horses, already upset, lurched into a trot.

Behind the wagon, apples littered the road in a long and rolling trail that did not end until the road curved away.

A fly had come to light on the spatter of Ruth's blood. I watched it drinking.

The other children were still lined up along the road. Quiet.

Henry and James came to stand with me. Henry, who

never did what I told him, said, "What should we do?"

Without Mrs. Taylor, we were all children now. Even the older boys, clustered behind the rest, looked small. I didn't see Andy. I didn't see Betty. At the time, I was glad they weren't around.

That's all I thought about them at the time.

I said, "Henry, run home and get someone."

Ours was not the nearest house, but it was the one where my mother was.

When Henry took off, James followed, and I didn't call him back, which would have done me no good in any event.

Then I fetched a pail of water at the well, poured it over the blood in the road, and went inside to wait.

Some of the other children came along. Most collected their things and went home. The littlest ones sat at their desks with their hands folded until someone came to fetch them. I sat at my desk, which was so much bigger without Ruth, put my head down, and cried.

I was waiting on the schoolhouse steps when my parents trundled down the road in our old truck and pulled up alongside the gully by the schoolhouse.

They took me close to them for a moment before my mother went to be with the other children.

My father bent to look me in the eye. "What happened, Annabelle?"

I'd stopped crying long before I ran out of tears, so they threatened now to start again.

"I don't know," I said. "I was standing just there"—I turned to point—"talking to Mr. Ansel. Ruth was a little behind me, scared of the grays. And then a rock hit her right here." I tapped my left eyelid. "And she fell down. Mrs. Taylor took Ruth away in her car."

My father straightened to look past me and the truck, at the road and the hill that rose up behind it. "Show me," he said.

So I walked around the truck and into the road. There was still a wet spot where I'd washed away Ruth's blood.

"Here," I said. "This is where Ruth was standing."

"Facing the hill? Mr. Ansel was headed down the hollow?"

"Yes, to market. See, the apples there, from how fast he went to tell Ruth's mother. Yes, she was standing there. And I was here," I said, moving to where I'd been, "and the horses right in front of me, and the wagon and Mr. Ansel here." I sketched a box with my hand.

"So the rock came from the hillside there?"

I looked up at the facing hill. It was steep, trees and bushes rooted everywhere they could root, ledges of slate all over the place, the gully below littered with fallen bits.

"It must have, I guess, since that's where Ruth was facing."

My father stood with his hands on his hips, considering the hillside. "So the wagon and the horses and you were all in between Ruth and the hill," he said.

I nodded. "That's right."

"Which means the rock couldn't have just fallen loose and bounced out of the gully or it would have hit the horses or the wagon before it hit Ruth," he said thoughtfully. "It had to have come down from higher up to clear all of you and hit her."

It wasn't a question, so I didn't answer it.

Far as I knew, no one had climbed that hill at recess, though the boys sometimes played King of the Mountain when school was over, grabbing hold of branches as they climbed, gaining footholds on the ledges and along the trunks of the trees. Rabbits and deer and boys had made zigzag paths that showed the easiest ways up and down.

"And you didn't see anyone up there when this happened?"

I shook my head. "I was looking at the horses and Mr. Ansel. And then I was looking at Ruth." And that was when my lips began to tremble.

"Okay, Annabelle," my father said, his hand on my head. "It's okay. We don't have to talk about this right now." But he turned and looked up the hill again, and I knew there would be more to come.

CHAPTER EIGHT

Ruth lost her eye. It was as simple as that.

I heard about it later that night from my mother. Most mothers might have waited until morning to deliver such news, but not my mother. She knew that I would have nightmares, regardless. Everything was about to get worse, and waiting to face it would not change that.

"It could have been me," I told my mother when she came and sat on the edge of my bed in the dark and told me that the doctor had not been able to repair Ruth's eye. That no one could have repaired it. The rock had ruined the parts that Ruth needed in order to see. That's how my mother put it.

"Yes," she said, stroking my hair. "It could have been you, Annabelle. But I think that rock was meant for Mr. Ansel or his grays or even his apples. Not you. Not Ruth."

"Why do you think that?"

My mother sighed. "Well, Mr. Ansel is German, Annabelle, and a lot of people around here are angry with the Germans. Have been since the last big war but especially now that we're in another one. It's not the first time someone has tried to do him harm, though before this they took it out on his crops or his truck. Broke windows. Put dead rats in his mailbox."

"But Mr. Ansel has lived here most of his life," I said.

"I know that. And you know that. But for some people it doesn't make any difference. He's the nearest thing they have, and they want someone to blame."

"Who does?"

My mother chewed on her lip. Didn't look at me. "People who have lost sons or fathers or brothers in the war. This one or the last one. People who fought in the war and came home angry or hurt. And really most everyone, since we all know soldiers over there right now, in harm's way, because of the Germans."

I thought about the gold stars on the flag at the church, one for each husband or brother or son who wouldn't come back to us. I thought about Toby: his silence and his guns.

"But how could anybody in the hollow know that Mr. Ansel would be passing through just then? They had to be on the hill already."

My mother shrugged. "I don't know, Annabelle. I only

71

know that no one was trying to hurt Ruth. What happened to her was just bad luck."

Which only made things worse. How was anyone supposed to stand up straight and open-eyed when luck could decide everything?

The next day started hard and got harder.

Breakfast was a quiet meal. Even my brothers were subdued. I didn't give a thought to anything but Ruth and what school would be like without her that day.

Despite myself, I began to cry, but as quietly as I could.

Aunt Lily said, "Oh, and what is it now that's worth such tears?"

My grandmother said, without looking at her, "Even Jesus wept, Lily," to which Aunt Lily replied, "And with good reason, which is more than I can say about this business."

"You mean Ruth losing her eye?" my mother said, some vinegar on her tongue. "You mean *that* business?"

At which Aunt Lily said, somewhat peevishly, "Well, if that's the root of it I suppose I misjudged the bloom."

Aunt Lily was always saying things like that, but admitting that she was wrong was a rare thing.

I didn't say anything at all.

James and Henry ate their breakfast like puppies, noisy and quick.

But my father drank his coffee slowly, his face grim, somewhere else.

"Stay away from the road and the hill at recess," he said before the boys and I went out the door. "Keep to the other side of the schoolhouse, by the woods. I mean to find out what happened to Ruth. Until then, don't go near the hill. Do you understand me?"

Yes, we nodded.

"Mind your sister," he told the boys, which was like telling them to fly to the moon.

But the boys, too, surprised me, waiting until we reached the fields on the downslope above Wolf Hollow before breaking away at a run to spook a grouse at the edge of the woods and then disappearing down the path into the trees without me.

When the path turned and I saw Betty sitting on a stump ahead, I was filled with regret that the reprieve I'd had was over and I was again to be her target.

But then I felt something else rise in its place.

I can't call it courage, since that's what people have when they are scared but do a hard thing regardless.

And I can't call it anger, though I'd been angry at Betty for the bruises she'd given me and the threats she'd made and the quail she'd killed.

I suppose I should have been both afraid and angry, but Ruth had lost her eye the day before, and what I felt now, looking at Betty's empty face, was more like indifference. She seemed, on that morning, insignificant and small, even as she stepped out in front of me.

"What?" I said impatiently.

She looked at me curiously. "Did you think I would leave you alone just because that crazy man told me to? Or because your little friend got hurt?"

"She got more than hurt," I said. "She lost her eye, Betty. Did you know that?"

Betty looked away. "My grandma told me. I'll bet someone was aiming for that filthy German. Not her."

"Mr. Ansel isn't filthy," I said. "You don't even know him."

She raised her eyebrows. "Way out here in these woods you might not know much, but I do. He might act all nice and jolly, but Germans are bullies who aim to take over the world. And they will if they can."

I noticed a long red thread of fresh scab across Betty's cheek, as if she'd been in brambles, and her socks were stuck all over with sticktights. I thought it odd that she'd been out in the rough so early in the day. And so soon after the ivy had laid her low.

"You're the only bully I know, Betty," I said. "But you're

going to leave me alone now. And not because Toby said so. And not because Ruth got hurt. You just will. I'm not going to give you anything. I'm not going to worry about you. I'm not going to run away from you. I'm just not. So you might as well leave me alone and get on with something else."

I waited, looking her full in the face, determined not to cut this short. I wanted to be done with Betty. If she was going to hurt me, she could hurt me right then and there, and I could finally do something about it before the day was out.

But she didn't do anything except spend another moment, thoughtful. And then she stepped aside.

I wasn't relieved. I wasn't happy about being left alone. I wasn't anything much. Just so sad, and tired in a way I'd never been before. I wanted nothing more than to hide in the hayloft in the barn and watch the rock doves napping in the rafters. To close my eyes and think about nothing at all. Not Ruth. Not Mr. Ansel. Not Germans. And not Betty Glengarry.

But if I couldn't retreat to the barn, school was the next best thing, and I gave myself over to my lessons. Andy didn't come to school that morning, so Benjamin reclaimed his customary seat; no one sat with me as Ruth usually did, and we all passed the morning quietly.

When recess came, I sat on the steps with some of the other girls, making crowns from long grass and supposing what

Ruth might be doing instead. The whole while I kept an eye on my brothers, but they didn't go near the road or the hill on the other side of it. As usual, they spent their time racing each other from here to there, making mud pies in the dirt around the well, and throwing rocks through the forks of trees.

Betty stood and watched them with her arms crossed. She never played. Usually she went off somewhere with Andy, but today, without him, she sat by herself and waited for recess to be over. Today she seemed more intent than usual. But she did not look at me once the whole time, so I paid her little attention in return.

And then, just as Mrs. Taylor called us back in to school, Andy came strolling into the yard.

Betty went to meet him halfway across the clearing, and they spent a moment together, talking, glancing at me as they did, before following us into school. I wondered what they were saying and what it had to do with me.

For the rest of the day, Andy and Betty passed notes and looks, ignored Mrs. Taylor when she asked them to join her at the chalkboard for arithmetic, and were the first two out the door when she dismissed us.

By the time I left the schoolhouse, they were nowhere in sight.

I didn't mind, then, when my brothers took off for home, racing each other up the hill and out of sight by the time I made it to the first turn in the path.

I heard them, though. First the sound of them racing away. The thud of their feet. A breathless *hey!* The mumble of loose pebbles on the path. Then a stretch of silence as they put more distance between us. And then a scream. And then Henry calling my name.

I ran to them up that hill as if it were flat ground.

I found Henry kneeling over James, who lay on his back in the path, crying, his forehead covered in blood.

I dropped to my knees beside them.

"I don't know what happened," Henry said. "James was ahead of me and he just suddenly fell back and started to cry."

"No, I didn't just fall down," James wailed, rolling onto his belly and pushing up onto his knees. He pointed along the path and there, just ahead, was a wire strung tight between two trees.

When Henry stood to have a closer look, I saw that the wire would have caught him in the neck if he'd been in the lead.

Henry ran his finger along the wire and jerked back. "It's sharp right here above the path," he said. "Like someone filed it."

He stepped into the brush and unwound the wire from one of the trees where it was anchored. Coiled the wire carefully and left it hanging from the tree on the other side of the path.

I used my sleeve to blot the blood from my brother's face. The cut was deep enough to bleed a lot, but it wasn't too bad.

"Come on," I said to James, helping him to his feet. "We'll get you fixed up just fine."

I took him by the hand and he let me, still blubbering. Henry went along in front, head up, as quiet and serious as a bull. From time to time he turned to look at me and James. At one point, as we crossed the fallow field on the brow of the hill, he turned and then stopped short. I looked back and saw Betty at the mouth of the path into the hollow, watching us.

"Not now," I said to Henry, who seemed to know what I meant. He stood stock-still and watched her as James and I hurried past. "Not now," I said again. And he turned to follow us home.

The wire was gone when I led my father back to where it had been.

"I know it was here," I said. "Just where that hump of root is. I made sure of it so I wouldn't forget."

My father stepped off the path and fingered the pale scar on the tree where the wire had taken a bite. There was another like it on the other side of the path. "You remembered right, Annabelle. This is where he tied the wire."

My father didn't get angry very often. My mother usually got angry first, so there wasn't much need for him to get involved. But this was different.

"Someone has a snake in him, and it's woken up," he said quietly.

I thought that was a very odd thing for him to say. He sounded a little like the reverend at our church or Aunt Lily when she got going, though he was not for the most part a churchy kind of man.

"But it's not a *he*, I don't think," I said. "Or if it is a *he* it's a *she*, too. Probably. At least I think it is. A *she*, I mean."

My father looked at me curiously. "Annabelle, it would be easier if you just spit it out."

"And I will. I just can't be sure because I didn't see her do it. But I am sure, I guess. It couldn't be anyone else. Unless it was Andy, too."

It was cold in the woods, the light going quickly, and I was happy to follow my father when he suddenly headed for the open fields above us. He took my hand as we crossed them, cut his stride down to half so I could keep up, and stopped at the top of the lane to pick a dozen apples for the sauce my mother would make that night. Then we went together down the lane through the trees that arched overhead, toward the house.

Only after we got inside and warm, spent a moment with James (my father calling him a "good little man") and another with my mother (who gave us both a long look), did he sit me down in the front room, quieter there than the kitchen, and asked me to say what was on my mind.

So I told him everything from the beginning. About Betty and her threats. About the cucumber-shaped bruise on my hip. How Andy and Betty had become friends so quickly and how furtive they had been for days now. About the quail and what Toby had done. About Andy coming late to school that morning and how the two of them had huddled in the schoolyard at recess, whispering.

I ran out of things to say and realized, to my dismay, that none of it sounded nearly as bad as it had felt at the time, though the memory of that quail's neck breaking would stay with me for the rest of my days. "She's a terrible bully," I said. "But I still don't know why I was so scared of her."

"Annabelle, why didn't you tell us right when she started up?"

"It happened in little bits, not all at once, and it wasn't easy to figure out what to do along the way." I felt like such a terrible fool. "Besides, she said she would hurt the boys if I told anyone. And then she went ahead and hurt James anyway when I wouldn't do what she said."

My father stood up and scrubbed his jaw with an open hand. "It's all right," he said. "I will take care of this now, Annabelle. Your mother and I. But from now on you tell us right away when you have a problem. Do you promise?"

I did. It was an easy promise to make. I had no intention of lying to my father or mother about anything else. I just didn't know how complicated things would become.

CHAPTER NINE

The next day was Saturday. No school. Chores, yes. But usually a chance, too, for some time on my own to spend as I pleased.

Not so, that Saturday.

"You and your mother and I will be paying a visit to the Glengarrys this afternoon," my father said when I sat down to breakfast. He used the voice that meant there would be no arguing.

"Do I have to go?" I said anyway.

My father nodded. "Something important shouldn't be said secondhand. But we'll be right there with you, and you'll feel better afterward. She won't have anything to hold over your head once it's all on the table."

That sounded right, but I still didn't want to go.

James sat across from me, moping over his eggs and worrying the edge of the white bandage across his forehead.

"This thing itches and it's dumb," he said. "I can't think right with it on me."

To which my mother had a quick answer, wrapping a bandanna around his head, pirate-style. "Now you look like Long John Silver," she said.

We knew a number of pirates, thanks to Robert Louis Stevenson and my grandmother, who read to us after supper most nights.

In no time at all, James was prancing around the house like a madman, crying "Ahoy, mateys," and thrusting and parrying with a wooden spoon until my mother shooed him out the door into the sunshine. Henry, too.

"Stay near," she called after them.

"We'll take them out to prune trees," my father said, pulling on his coat, my grandfather with him. Christmas season was nearly upon us, and it was time to start shaping the small spruces we grew for selling. My father did the pruning while my grandfather sat in the truck with a dog or two and supervised the operation. The year before, my father had let the boys practice on a crooked spruce, and they'd shaped it into an excellent toothpick. This year, the boys were again in charge of gathering what fell in the rows and bundling the best of it for wreaths.

The house settled a little with them gone.

We tidied up the breakfast things and began our Saturday chores, my mother ironing in the kitchen, the air charged with the smell of hot clean cotton, the sound of the iron striking the board. My grandmother sat at one end of the big tiger-oak table, mending socks and patching elbows.

I pared apples for pies, doing my best to make one long, curling ribbon from each apple. Whenever I fed the peels to the horses, they didn't seem to appreciate my efforts, but I liked things pretty if they could be.

Aunt Lily, restless without work or church, did her best to taint our Saturdays so we were as miserable as she was.

"It would be quicker if you weren't trying to do that," she told me, picking up a long peel at one end and bouncing the coil until it broke.

I almost offered to share the chore with her, but Aunt Lily didn't have much of a knack for housework.

"Did you send in Toby's film?" I asked her.

She lifted her chin sharply. "Of course I did, Annabelle. Supervising the mail is a great duty. Once it is in my hands, it gets sorted and sent with no nonsense whatsoever."

"Oh, I know," I said. "I didn't mean anything."

Aunt Lily gave a little nod. "You shall have the photographs in no time at all," she said. "Though I'm not sure why that man has our camera or any right to what is ours, all that expensive film. Sending it in, getting it back, and so on and so forth. Making more work for us to do, and for what?"

My mother shook her head at the "ours." She had won the camera and everything that went with it. "I'm going to visit Ruth," she said to me. "Do you want to come along?"

Well, I didn't. The very thought of it scared me. But "Yes," I said, "I do."

And when the ironing and the paring and the washing up were done, I put on my jacket and hat and went with my mother out the door.

Ruth lay in her bed, the covers tucked up across her thin chest. She wore a black silk eye patch. Green-and-yellow bruising seeped from beneath it and across her cheek. Beyond that, she was as pale as February.

"Hi, Ruth," I said after our mothers had spent a little time fussing over her and then settled themselves in the sitting room for a talk. "Does it hurt?"

Ruth nodded slowly. She had not yet said anything but "Thank you, ma'am," when my mother gave her a twist of wax paper filled with molasses drops.

"Are you coming back to school soon?"

Ruth started to shake her head but then stopped. "My parents won't let me go back there," she said, looking away from me. "I have to go to a school in Sewickley now."

I was stunned. "All that way into the city?"

"My father works there, Annabelle. We only live out here because my grandpa left us this house when he died. We never meant to stay so long, but it was nice here. Quiet." She looked back at me and I could see that she was crying. "But we're going to sell the house and move to the city now."

I had spent years growing up with Ruth, one of the sweetest, gentlest people I knew, and I began to cry, too. "I'm so sorry you got hurt," I said.

Ruth stiffened. "I didn't get hurt," she said. "Someone hurt me."

I wiped my face. "Did you see anything?"

"Not really. Something moved on the hillside and I looked up and that's why the rock hit me so square in the eye. If I'd been looking down just a little . . ." She brought her knees up and crossed her wrists under her chin. "They say I'll get used to it. But I don't think I will."

"Time to go, Annabelle," my mother said from the doorway. "Ruth needs her rest."

When I said good-bye, I didn't even hug Ruth or wish

her well. I didn't know that this would be the last time I'd ever see her.

The visit to the Glengarrys was worse.

It was strange to sit between my parents on a threadbare settee in the Glengarrys' front room while Betty and her grandparents sat on kitchen chairs arranged in a line across from us. They sat higher than we did, and their faces were serious, but my parents were calm and warm on either side of me.

"I'm glad for the chance to thank you," Mr. Glengarry began. "For the jewelweed. By the time I got home from Ohio, Betty was already on the mend. We're very grateful for your help."

"And we're glad to give it, always," my mother said. The "but" hovered on her lips.

My father said, "We want to talk with you about what's been going on at school."

"So do we," Mr. Glengarry said. "Betty has told us some very serious things about what happened to Ruth."

"To Ruth?" my mother said. "We're not here about Ruth. We're here about what happened to James, our youngest. And to Annabelle."

The Glengarrys looked puzzled.

Betty simply stared straight at me, unmoving.

Everyone in the room knew why Betty had come to live in the country, so I did not expect to surprise anyone when I said, "Betty told me that if I didn't bring her things, she would hurt me and my brothers. Which she did. First me, with a stick, twice, and then a quail she caught, and then yesterday, my little brother, with a sharp wire strung across the path to school. But I think Andy Woodberry helped with that part."

It came out faster than the silence that followed it.

"Betty?" Her grandma looked torn right down the middle, one half resigned, the other a little hopeful. "Did you do these things?"

Betty shook her head. "I never did," she said. "I wouldn't do that."

"But you did, and you know you did," I insisted. "Even though I brought you a penny and tried to be your friend."

My mother put a hand on my knee to hush me. "Annabelle wouldn't lie about such things," she said.

"But Betty would?" Mr. Glengarry didn't sound angry quite, but I could see where this was headed. I imagined that my own grandfather would stand up for me no matter what I'd done.

"Ask Toby if you don't believe me," I said. "He saw what happened when I gave her the penny. She threw it away and hit me with a stick, and I have the bruise to prove it. And

88

when she killed the quail, Toby told her to leave me alone. But she didn't. She's the one who strung that wire. I know it."

"Hush, now, Annabelle," my mother said. "It's all right."

"Toby?" Mr. Glengarry said. "That wild man?" He looked at his granddaughter. "Tell them what you told us."

When she didn't say anything, her grandmother put an arm around Betty and said, "It's okay, Honey. You don't need to be afraid now."

Betty tipped her head to one side, just a little, her eyes still on me. "I saw Toby on the hillside up above where Ruth got hurt," she said. "But he scares me so bad I was afraid to say anything about it."

I remembered Ruth telling me she'd seen something moving on the hill just before the rock hit her. But it couldn't have been Toby.

"You're the one who's scary, Betty," I said. "Toby didn't have anything to do with all that. Toby would never hurt Ruth."

"He surely wasn't aiming at her," said Mr. Glengarry. "He was aiming at the German."

Mr. Ansel. The German.

Mr. Glengarry had lost a brother in the first big war, and he was one of the people who didn't speak to Mr. Ansel. "Toby's crazy because of what the Germans did to him. If anyone would be throwing rocks at a German, it would be Toby."

"I didn't see Toby," I said, "and I was right there in the road with Ruth." To Betty, I said, "You weren't anywhere around when she got hurt, Betty, so how come you're the only one who saw him?"

"I was up in the belfry," Betty said. "Andy wanted to show me the school bell when everyone went out to recess. There's a little window up there, looks right out onto the road and the hill. I saw it happen better than you ever could from down below."

My mother leaned forward a little. "But you didn't say anything about it until now?" If anyone was a friend to Toby, it was my mother. It was clear that she didn't believe Betty, but I, too, had kept a secret because I was afraid of someone bigger and stronger than I was, and she knew that.

"I thought he would hurt me if I did," Betty said.

I was stunned at how small she sounded. She, who had turned the tables with no effort at all.

"Andy's not afraid of Toby," I said. "How come he didn't say anything?"

"Because I was the only one who saw what happened. Andy was on the other side of the belfry, messing around with a swallow's nest, and by the time he made it over to the window, Toby was gone. I didn't tell him what I'd seen. I was afraid Toby might hurt Andy, too."

She sounded so scared that I almost believed her.

"What about the wire across the path?" I said. "Toby wouldn't hurt James."

"Maybe not, but I take that path, too," she said. "Maybe Toby meant it for me."

"That's enough now," Mr. Glengarry said. "Toby's crazy. Everybody knows that. And you can't expect anything but crazy business from a crazy man."

"I don't blame Betty one little bit for being afraid of Toby," Mrs. Glengarry said. She was a quiet woman and I was surprised to hear the grit in her voice, but here was a chance to believe that Betty was nothing but a pigtailed girl in a blue jumper afraid of a bad man who carried guns wherever he went.

"Perhaps not." My mother rose to her feet. "But if anyone threatens Annabelle again, there won't be any more talking about it."

I wasn't sure what she meant by that, but when my father took me by the hand and we stood next to her, I felt like a giant. Like when I stood on our hilltop looking down into Wolf Hollow. Or when I held a bird's egg in my hand.

After we got home, my parents spent some time in the yard, talking. I went inside and straight up to my room.

My steady world was spinning, and with each turn of the pinwheel, I became more confused.

I didn't believe that Toby was crazy. Sad, maybe. Quiet. Odd, even, to choose a life alone, sleeping in a smokehouse, walking the hills day after day. But not crazy. Not dangerous-crazy.

And besides, why would Toby throw a rock from a hillside when two girls and two horses stood below? If Toby wanted to hurt Mr. Ansel, he had chances every day, all over the place, when there wouldn't be any girls or horses standing by.

Toby was a man who wouldn't even shoot a sleeping deer. Who took pictures of mayapples. And gave me back a penny when he didn't need to. And had never hurt anyone, anyone, since coming back from that terrible war. Not that I knew of.

I didn't believe Toby was crazy. Not even a little bit. And I didn't believe he would hurt Mr. Ansel, German or not.

But if Betty and Andy had been in the belfry, they couldn't have been on that hillside. They couldn't have thrown that rock.

I lay on my bed and thought my thoughts until I heard my mother calling me down to help get supper started. And a little beyond that.

"You must have enough wool by now to knit a sweater," my grandmother said as we washed and peeled potatoes together at the sink.

"What wool?" I sloshed a potato in the wash water until it came away white.

"You've been gathering wool this whole time, Annabelle. Not a word out of you."

I shrugged. "Just thinking about Ruth."

"A terrible thing to happen to anyone, let alone a sweet girl like her."

"But you don't think Toby did it, even by accident, do you?"

By now everyone in the house knew about the conversation at the Glengarrys' that afternoon.

Aunt Lily had sniffed and said, "That Toby has always smelled like brimstone to me."

Henry had said, "Naw, Toby's not like that."

James had said, "Avast, there, matey." Which we took to mean no.

My grandfather had shaken his head and mumbled something about a sheep in wolf's clothing.

I already knew how my mother felt. My father . . . I wasn't sure. He hadn't said a word on our way home from the Glengarrys' house. And, once home, he'd spoken only to my mother and then gone straightaway to his chores.

"Oh, I don't know what I think," my grandma said, cutting a potato so thin I could see light through the slice. Hers were the best scalloped potatoes in the county. "Toby is odd, I have to say. And those guns of his give me pause. But I've never seen him act rough with anyone. And I've never heard of him speaking ill of the Germans, including Mr. Ansel."

"Well, Toby doesn't speak much about anything," I had to admit.

"No, he does not. But I've always wanted people to judge me by my actions, and I hope I can do the same for him, who has never done me wrong. Or my family, neither."

My father came in to supper that night pink with evening but smelling like soot.

"I spent some time with Toby this afternoon," he said in the middle of eating my mother's ham, my grandmother's potatoes, and my cauliflower, which James referred to as "little white trees" and rarely ate.

We all looked at my father and waited. I, especially, wondered what Toby had had to say about the goings-on of the past week.

"I did most of the talking," he said. "Knocked on the door, Toby answered, asked me in. There was no place to sit but on the one chair and I would not sit if he couldn't, so we both stood there looking at each other like a couple of goats."

My father didn't admire goats very much. I, if lazy, was a little goat. If stupid, a goat. If dirty, a goat. And the rest of us, too.

We waited. He would not have mentioned the visit at all if there were not more to tell.

"That shack of his is a hard place," he said, "though he's nicened it up a bit. Not much of a bed, more like a nest. Pine boughs covered with burlap. No pillow. An old army blanket. The one chair, castoff. A fire pit dug in one corner with just a hole for a vent. Odds and ends on the hooks above. But . . ." And here he stopped. Sat back in his chair. Ran a hand over his jaw. "There were pictures everywhere. On all four walls. Of the orchards. The woods. Sky all by itself in lots of them, at sundown."

He paused for a moment. "They were beautiful, and I wanted to see them all, but the light was going, and I didn't want to presume. He hadn't invited me, and he seemed a little nervous to have me there. I don't imagine he gets many visitors."

I couldn't remember my father ever saying so much in one stretch.

"I told him about what the Glengarrys had said. What Betty had said. I asked him if he'd been on that hillside. And he said he had no reason to throw a rock at anyone, German or not."

My grandfather said, "If anyone had a reason to throw a rock at a German, it might be Toby."

95

"Or anyone who lost kin over there," my mother said sharply. "Of which there are plenty."

"And then he said something strange," my father said. "He said, and I think I've got this right, 'They made scratches on the Turtle Stone.' And he didn't say anything after that, except to ask that you, Annabelle, bring him his pictures as soon as they come in."

Aunt Lily waggled her fork at me. "Our camera. Our film. *His* pictures. I like that."

But I was wondering about the Turtle Stone, a big boulder in Wolf Hollow shaped like a turtle's shell and threaded through with quartz in something of a grid, also like a turtle's shell. Everyone knew about the Turtle Stone. It was in a little clearing as if the trees had not dared get too close, and the ground around it was covered with ferns and flowering weeds.

It was a pretty place but serious, too. We always figured that the Indians had used it for ceremonies. If we hadn't had a church for our ceremonies, we probably would have chosen the Turtle Stone, too.

CHAPTER TEN

Church the next morning was much as it always was, except that the Glengarrys, in their pew three back from ours, did not greet us as they usually did. I was sorry about that, but not very.

My father had been right when he'd said I'd feel better after speaking my piece, and I didn't mind giving up a Sunday smile from the Glengarrys in the bargain.

Betty, in a gingham shift over a white blouse with a Peter Pan collar, looked as sweet as a snap pea, but her eyes gave her away.

I focused instead on the purple and yellow mums clustered around the altar and the empty cross above it.

The choir warbled out the hymns as usual, Mr. Simmons through his mighty nose, Mrs. Lancaster with a bigger hitch in her voice than our flatbed, and we all sang along in our various ways.

Reverend Kinnell spoke at great length about the changing of the seasons, but I could not for the life of me make much sense of it. I was very grateful for the tiny pencil and offerings envelope stashed next to the hymnal on the pew-back in front of me. I couldn't draw worth a hill of beans, but trying helped me pass the time. My grandfather, sitting next to me, looked envious as I spent much of the sermon drawing a horse.

"That's a fine dog, Annabelle," he whispered to me.

When my mother took the envelope to add some coins for the collection, she smiled at the dog-horse. "I hope the reverend likes your offering, Annabelle," she said.

So everything was fine, I thought, and whatever problems we had could wait for us to catch up with them.

But, as it turned out, they caught up with *us* when we left the church and found the constable waiting outside, the Glengarrys with him.

The constable didn't wear a badge or carry a weapon, but the state police barracks were in Pittsburgh and the nearest jail or courthouse was just as far away; so the constable took care of things as he could and called in the troops when they were needed, which was never, as far as I knew.

We all liked him. Constable Oleska. He had a big face, red cheeks, not much hair, and an easy laugh. But one time at the county fair I'd seen him wrap his arms around a farmer who'd had too much hard cider and was acting stupid. Constable Oleska held him in place as if he were nothing but a corn shock, until the farmer calmed down and went home to bed. So people took the constable seriously when he chose to be stern.

He looked stern now.

"Good morning, folks," he said. "I need a word, John. Sarah."

My father opened the door to our truck and shepherded my grandparents inside.

To my brothers and me, he made a shooing motion and we obliged him by scrambling up into the back, but we huddled as close to the conversation as we could.

I couldn't hear everything they said, but I caught Toby's name and Ruth's and Mr. Ansel's. Betty did some of the talking, which made me mad, but my parents were there to speak for me, and I resigned myself to that.

My mother's voice was most audible, since she quickly became upset with what the Glengarrys were saying.

"Whatever happened to innocent until proven guilty?" she said, a fair bit of heat in her voice. "And letting a person live however he likes?" She had her fists on her hips. "Let's not be throwing the baby out with the bath-water."

Which was confusing to me, since there was no baby involved in this as far as I could tell. Nor any bathwater, either.

My father put a hand on her shoulder, but she ignored him. "Toby may be strange, but that's the end of it. You might make him more than strange if you back him into a corner when he hasn't done anything wrong. Besides, you can't lock up a man because a girl says she saw him on a hillside. And a girl who's been up to no good, at that."

And then everyone was talking too loudly and none of them in turn. My mother had clearly tired of the whole business and climbed into the back of the truck with us. My father got behind the wheel, starting the engine, and calling, "Lily!" out the window.

But my aunt stayed another moment, talking to the constable, nodding her birdlike head to what he replied, before heading for her own car. I did not like the look on her face. Something too close to happy, which was rare enough for Aunt Lily and odder still, given the circumstances.

Sunday dinner was usually a matter of saying grace and eating what we were served. Little conversation. Redding up afterward (while Aunt Lily went to her room to spend the afternoon in prayer and reflection . . . though sometimes a dance tune drifted from under her door).

People occasionally came to call on Sundays. More often, we spent the day slowly, quietly. Glad for a little peace and rest.

But this Sunday was not like that.

"I want you to stay far away from Betty Glengarry at school tomorrow," my mother said to my brothers and me after dinner as she dished out apple pie and poured cream over it. "Don't go near her. Don't talk to her. And tell Mrs. Taylor if Betty does anything worrisome. Anything at all."

"And us, too," my father said, "when you get home. No more secrets."

"Well, honestly," Aunt Lily said. "Annabelle, don't you think you might have been exaggerating a bit? Betty seems like a sweet, God-fearing girl to me, and she's brave enough to let us know what Toby's done, even though he's the most frightening thing in this county."

"She hit me hard enough to leave a black bruise the size of a cucumber," I said. "No way I could exaggerate black."

Aunt Lily sat up straighter. "Thou shalt not bear false witness against thy neighbor," she said sharply.

But though it had been some time since Betty had swung that stick, I stood up and bared my hip right there in front of everyone and let them see the mark that was still visible. Still ugly enough.

Aunt Lily looked away. She didn't say another word for the rest of the meal.

After dinner was over and the redding-up was done, my mother gathered the fixings for a poultice and made it while I watched. A handful of Russian comfrey leaves from her kitchen garden and boiling water, mashed into a hot paste, spooned into a clean rag, folded up into a neat square. She took me to my room, laid me down on my side, and arranged the poultice on my bruise.

"It doesn't hurt anymore," I said.

"Well, it hurts me to know it's there," she said. "This will clear it up altogether."

What felt best was having my mother sit on the edge of my bed, her hand over the poultice to keep it warm.

"I didn't bear false witness," I said. "I wouldn't do that."

"Oh, I know, Annabelle. Aunt Lily thinks she knows more than she does. Enough about that now."

We sat quietly, and I felt a great distance between us and the sound of my brothers downstairs, their Sunday pitch imperfect, noisy as any weekday.

"What's going to happen to Toby?" I asked.

My mother sighed. "Well, Constable Oleska doesn't have enough information to call the troopers and have Toby arrested, which is what the Glengarrys want him to do. He can't dismiss what Betty said, but he can't arrest Toby on the strength of that alone. Can't arrest him in any event, since that's for the troopers to decide and do. So he said he's going to talk to Andy about Betty's story, about being in the belfry. And he's going down to see Toby, too. And maybe come talk to you a little, about that other business with Betty. And try to figure out who strung that wire across the path. All that, though I don't know in what order. Maybe talk to Toby tonight, even, or early tomorrow. I just don't know, Annabelle. But for now all he wants is to talk to people, find out what's what."

I tucked my hands under my cheek, tried to picture the constable knocking on the door to Toby's smokehouse, imagined the look on Toby's face when he opened the door and found trouble on the other side.

"I don't believe what they're saying about Toby. He's not like that."

"Nor do I, Annabelle. But Constable Oleska is a fair man. I don't think he'll do anything but talk for now."

Which, I feared, might itself be too much. Toby had been a wanderer. I expected he might right now be thinking about leaving our hills for somewhere new.

CHAPTER ELEVEN

Monday came.

There was no sign of Toby as the boys and I walked to school. It was raining lightly, threatening more, and blowing cold, but I had still hoped to see him on a hilltop, just to know he hadn't left.

Perhaps I would go down to his shack after school. Not to bother him, just to see if I could spy him sheltering there, out of the rain. Though he walked in all weathers and seasons and would likely do so today, too.

First, though, I would go to school. My parents always told me that school was my most important job. I knew, with two brothers, that I would never farm this land, and I wanted and had to grow up an educated woman.

Today, I would learn some arithmetic, no doubt, and

a few state capitals, why we fought the wars we fought, what Anne of Green Gables would get up to next, and why I shouldn't mix bleach with ammonia. But first on my list was what Andy had to say.

My parents had told me to stay away from Betty, but they had not told me to avoid Andy. He was a bully, for sure, but I meant to ask him about the belfry and the taut-wire across the path.

Toby had said, "They made scratches on the Turtle Stone," and I wondered if he meant Betty and Andy . . . if that was where they'd sharpened the wire that had cut James. I pictured one of them on each side of the Turtle Stone, the ends of the wire wrapped around stick handles so they could pull it to and fro, like a two-man saw, honing it sharp.

What I couldn't fathom was how they had thought to do that. Or why they'd actually done the thing. Even a wolf has reasons for what it does. Even a snake makes sense when it eats a robin's egg.

By the time we got to the schoolhouse, it was raining in earnest. We three had worn oilcloth ponchos, hoods up, and boots, so we were plenty dry and warm, but many of the other children came in soaked and shivering. For the first time that season, Mrs. Taylor lit a fire in the stove at the front of the room and gave the wettest of her students a chance to dry out before lessons began.

"Goodness, what happened to you?" she asked James, bending low to look at the bandage on his forehead.

When James glanced my way, I shook my head. "Pirates," he said.

Mrs. Taylor nodded. "I thought so." She returned to the front of the room.

"Those of you who aren't too wet, come on up here," she called, and so my brothers and I went forward, a few others, too, and I wondered what she had in mind for such a mixed bunch.

Not state capitals, as it turned out.

"I want to talk to you about what happened to Ruth," she said, glancing at the door. I turned to look, but it was shut and no one had come in. I realized, then, that both Andy and Betty were absent again.

I wasn't surprised about Andy. On such a rainy day he would be forgiven many of his chores at home, so why bother with school? Betty, I thought, might be at this moment leading the charge against Toby. I pictured her practicing both prim and proper, aiming for innocent, and probably succeeding with those who didn't know her.

"Annabelle?" I turned back to Mrs. Taylor. The other children were looking at me. "I asked you how you were doing. I'm sure it wasn't easy to see Ruth get hurt like that."

"It wasn't," I said. "But I'm okay."

She talked for a little while about the importance of trusting people, telling them about the things that bothered us.

"If any of you saw Toby on that hillside, or anyone else for that matter, or anything odd that day, you should tell someone. Me, your parents, Reverend Kinnell. Someone who can help you do the right thing."

I raised my hand. "Who told you that Toby was on the hillside?"

"I heard about it at church yesterday," she said. "From the Glengarrys."

I thought about that for a moment. "So you know that Betty is the one saying Toby threw that rock?"

Mrs. Taylor nodded. "Yes, I heard that."

"Then can I please go up to the belfry so I can see what there is to see out that window?"

To which Mrs. Taylor, clearly baffled, said, "Why would you want to do that?"

"Because Betty said she was in the belfry with Andy at recess when she saw Toby through the window, on the hillside."

Mrs. Taylor said, very slowly, "Betty claims they were up there the day Ruth got hurt?"

I nodded. The other children listened to all this more attentively than they ever listened during lessons.

Mrs. Taylor stood up, went to a door at the back of the room. It didn't open when she tried it. She came back to us then, deep in thought.

"All right," she said. "Go on back to your seats and read the assignments I've written on the chalkboard."

She joined the children drying out around the stove. From my desk I could hear her telling them to trust people. To tell the truth.

While I read about the Spanish-American War, I listened for the door to open. For Betty to walk in. But she didn't.

It was still raining at recess, so we stayed inside and played marbles and cat's cradle. Before calling us back to our lessons, Mrs. Taylor had us do a long series of jumping jacks. "To make you strong," she said, though I knew what the afternoon would be like if the boys, especially, didn't wear themselves out a little first.

As we were returning to our desks, the door finally opened, but it was Andy who came in, not Betty.

He tipped off his hood and shook all over like a dog as he looked around the schoolhouse. "Where's Betty?" he said. When no one answered him, he said, more loudly, "Mrs. Taylor. Where's Betty?"

She turned from the chalkboard. "I have no idea, Andy. She didn't come to school this morning. I wonder if she might be sick."

Andy pulled his hood back up over his head. Left without another word.

Mrs. Taylor stood where she was, looking long at where he'd been.

"Settle down everyone," she finally said. "Time for lessons."

At the end of the day, as my brothers were putting on their rain boots, Mrs. Taylor took me aside and said, "I'd like to come see your parents after suppertime, Annabelle. Do you think that would be all right?"

I was startled by the very idea of it. "Did I do something wrong? Or my brothers?"

"Oh no, Annabelle. Nothing like that. I just want to talk with your parents for a few minutes."

"Well, then, sure," I said.

I didn't want to be rude, but I was curious: "Do you have a telephone at your house, Mrs. Taylor?"

"I do. Why?"

"Because we do, too." I hoped I didn't sound fresh. "You could just call them up, if you want."

Mrs. Taylor gave me a little smile. "I could. But . . ." She paused to choose her words. "Well, I'm sure you know that Mrs. Gribble is, sometimes, a little . . . curious . . . when she puts a call through."

Ah.

Annie Gribble lived in a small house that we passed on our way to market. I'd only been there once, to drop off a bushel of peaches at canning time, but she'd invited us in for a glass of lemonade, my father and me, and I'd been fascinated by the switchboard that dominated her front room like a loom strung with thin black snakes.

She sat there all day long and made connections between the families in our hills that had acquired telephones. To use ours, we had to ring up Annie and tell her where to place the call. And she had a habit of listening in to hear news that she thought other people really ought to know.

We were used to the idea by now. Nobody dared tell a secret over the telephone, for fear that Annie was eavesdropping. But Annie made hay out of even small things, so we'd learned to start a conversation with the most boring of our news, hoping that she'd be more easily distracted by another customer calling in for a connection.

Whatever Mrs. Taylor wanted to talk about, it wasn't meant for Annie's ears.

"Do you want me to tell them you're coming by?" I said.

"I would appreciate it," Mrs. Taylor said.

I pulled on my boots and tried to tie the laces of James's hood under his chin, but he tossed his head like a young horse and galloped out of the school into the rain before I could do a proper job. Henry followed him, and they both did a mud dance across the sloppy schoolyard before gaining drier ground in the woods.

I was not in the mood to walk home alone, in the cold and wet, but I saw no alternative until Mrs. Taylor called me back. "Annabelle, I could come for a visit now if you think that would be all right, and you could ride with me."

I rarely had a chance to ride in a car as nice as hers. More importantly, it would be warm and dry.

"I imagine my father will be at the house or close by on a day like this," I said. "And I'm sure my mother will be there. So now would be okay, I guess."

I followed her to the car and climbed into the backseat, feeling a little like a queen, until I realized that I was sitting where Ruth had been.

It was a slow and careful ride to the farm, the roads awash in some places, but we got there without mishap.

"You go on in and make sure it's a good time for a visit," Mrs. Taylor said. "I'll wait here."

So I did that, and my mother hurried past me to open the door and beckon Mrs. Taylor inside.

"Mrs. Taylor, come in, please," my mother said, in her Sunday voice. She called most people by their Christian names, but not the minister, the doctor, the constable, or the teacher.

"Thank you," Mrs. Taylor said, trying to shed as much

rainwater from her bonnet as she could before she stepped inside.

"Oh, don't fuss about that," my mother said. "You'd be the only one who did. Annabelle," she said to me before I could take off my poncho, "run to the barn and fetch your father."

So back outside I went. And laughed out loud when I saw my brothers pull up short at the sight of me as they slithered down the muddy lane. "Mrs. Taylor gave me a ride in her car!" I yelled to them and, laughing still, headed for the barn.

Our old barn taught me one of the most important lessons I was ever to learn: that the extraordinary can live in the simplest things.

Each season meant a world refashioned inside its stalls and storerooms.

Pockets of warmth in winter, the milk cows and draft horses like furnaces, their heat banked by straw bedding and new manure.

In spring, swallows fledged from muddy nests wedged in crannies overhead, and kittens fresh and soft staggered between hooves and attacked the tails of tackle hanging from stable pegs.

Come summer, yellow jackets nested in the straw,

old oats sprouted through the floorboards, Houdini hens laid eggs in odd places where they might yield chicks, and dusty sunlight striped the air like bridges to somewhere else.

But I loved the barn in fall, especially, when I'd often find my father there, mending wagon wheels, oiling the joints of wagon parts, and sometimes—as on that November day—napping in the hayloft, snoring softly in the dim, blue light.

"Mrs. Taylor is here to see you," I said softly into his ear while the rain thrummed on the tin roof just above our heads and the horses stamped for their oats below us. "Wake up."

My father roused suddenly from continents away. "What?" he said, sitting up in the hay.

"Mrs. Taylor is here to see you," I repeated. I sat back on my heels. "You have straw in your hair."

He pawed it away, I plucked off a stubborn bit, and we both rose and climbed down the hayloft ladder, my father clearing his throat and shaking the sleep from his head.

"I was just having a little rest," he said as we walked abreast down the dim stairs into the stable below. He ran his hands through his hair. "Mrs. Taylor, you say?"

"She wants to talk with you and Mother."

He looked at me sharply. "What did James do?"

"Nothing. Henry neither. I don't know what it's about, but I think it has something to do with Betty."

My father sighed as he pulled his hood up over his head. "I've had about my fill of all that," he said. And walked straight out into the hard rain.

By the time we pulled off our boots and hung up our wet ponchos, my mother had made coffee and put some oatmeal cookies on a plate. Mrs. Taylor was waiting for us in the front room, perched on the edge of a chair, her hands folded, as if we had bad news for her.

I was afraid it would be the other way around.

"I'm not sure Annabelle needs to be part of this," she said hesitantly once we were all seated.

"Well, I'm not sure what 'this' is," my mother said, "but if it has anything to do with what happened to Ruth, she really ought to hear it. She's been right in the middle of that mess from the start."

Mrs. Taylor nodded. "If you think it's all right." She spent a moment quietly, unfocused, and then she looked up and said, "I understand that Betty claims she was in the belfry looking out the window when she saw Toby throw the rock that hit Ruth."

My father nodded. "That's what she says."

"Only that can't be right." Mrs. Taylor sighed. "A few days before Ruth got hurt, I caught Betty and Andy up in the belfry at recess. I shooed them out and then I locked the door that leads to the belfry stairs. It was still locked today when I tried it. And I have the only key right here." She patted her pocketbook.

"One more lie," my mother said quietly.

"One more *big* lie," I said, trailing off as everyone turned to look at me. "What? It's true. Betty didn't see Toby do a thing. Betty's a bully. She's just mad at him because he told her to leave me alone."

My father took my hand. "It's all right, Annabelle. You aren't wrong. Betty had that lie already on her tongue because she'd been up in the belfry before and knew just what to say."

Mrs. Taylor sighed. "That does seem to fit."

"Would you please go tell that to Constable Oleska?" I said.

She nodded. "I will," she said. "But I wanted to come see you first. The Glengarrys are my friends, and I didn't want to make an accusation without talking it out first."

"No accusation about it," my father said. "Just information. The constable will do with it what he can."

For days I'd been feeling as tense as a banjo string, twanging every time some new problem arose, but there were also moments of relief, like this one. Finally, maybe, people were beginning to understand what kind of person Betty really was.

Mrs. Taylor stood up and we with her. "Betty didn't

come to school today. I imagine she's home sick. Perhaps I should go by and speak with the Glengarrys first before I see the constable."

My mother shook her head. "We've been in your shoes, and lately. It won't do any good. They are set on the idea that Betty has done nothing wrong."

Mrs. Taylor nodded. "I expect you're right about that. Betty's an . . . odd girl, but she's their granddaughter."

We didn't talk about the rest of it, how badly she had bullied me, how I suspected she and Andy had hurt James. But the lid was off, the worms were rearing their slick little heads, and they would soon be spilling out with their mucky secrets.

I can't say I was glad, exactly, but I wasn't sorry.

CHAPTER TWELVE

We were all in bed that night, the house dark, when we were awakened by pounding at our door. The dogs that generally slept in the woodshed were by now having a loud conversation with someone outside, and we could hear him talking back to them firmly.

The rain had stopped, but the night outside our door was thick with wet air, and Constable Oleska looked like he wore a layer of spiderweb over his black raincoat. One or two dogs continued to question him, but they quieted down at a single word from my father, who stood in the doorway in his night things, my mother behind him tightening her robe, while I peeked around her, my brothers behind me, and Aunt Lily came marching to join us, her hair in rollers, her face angry.

"And what is all this about now?" she said.

I imagined my grandparents sitting up in their bed, hoping they wouldn't have to join the fray.

"Very sorry to wake you, John, Sarah . . . hello, Lily," Constable Oleska said. "I know it's late, but can I come in for a minute?"

"Of course," my father said. He stepped back to let the constable by.

"I wouldn't have come so late, but I'm afraid I couldn't wait until morning," the constable said. "Betty Glengarry has gone missing."

"Missing?" my father said.

"You'd better come on in and sit," my mother said.

"I'll bet she got eaten by a bear," James said, his hair sticking out in all directions.

"You, boys, back to bed," my father said. "Now."

When they hesitated, Aunt Lily took them in hand with a sharp word and a set mouth. "Bed, your father said." As if they were wayward sheep, she poked and prodded them out of the room.

I, it seemed, would be allowed to stay.

For a while, being included in these conversations had made me feel tall. Now I was ready to be eleven again and back up in bed like my brothers. I could feel myself tightening up as before and wished that whoever was doing the tuning would have pity. None of this was fun.

"Please. Come on now. Sit," my mother said.

When the constable looked down at his mud-caked boots, water streamed from the divot in his hat. "I'm a mess, Sarah."

But my mother took him by the arm and led him to a chair at the kitchen table.

"You're cold right through and wet," she said as she put some supper coffee on the stove to warm. "A little mud won't matter."

We all took a seat as Aunt Lily returned to the kitchen. "You, too," she said to me. "Back to bed. This is no talk for children," as if my parents were not sitting right there alongside me.

"Leave her be, Lily," my father said. "Annabelle may know more about this than we do."

The constable took off his hat and laid it on his knees. "Mrs. Taylor came to see me about the whole belfry business," he said, smoothing his hair flat. "We talked it through, I saw where things were headed, and I had made up my mind to visit the Glengarrys in the morning . . . when here they came, knocking at the door." He rubbed his hands to warm them. "It was dark by then. Betty hadn't come home from school, and they were worried. More so when Mrs. Taylor told them Betty had never come to school in the first place."

I nodded. "We thought she must be sick."

Constable Oleska shook his head. "No, she left for school as always, rain or not. Her grandma dressed her for the wet and then watched her go down the lane and disappear, headed toward Wolf Hollow. Same as ever."

My mother got up to pour him some coffee. "No sign at all of where she went?"

"In this weather? The whole world's mud and flood."

"Then what?" my father said. "If there's something you need from us . . ."

"Toby's gone," the constable said. "First thing I did was go down to his shack to find out if he'd seen her. Not—" he said suddenly, his hands up, "not to suggest he'd done anything wrong. First time I went to see him, after Ruth got hurt, I found him outside the shack, chopping wood. When I told him what Betty was saying about him, Toby got a look on his face, and I have to say . . . I didn't like it. And I wasn't happy that he had an ax in his hand at the time. But he didn't say a word or do a thing. Just went back to his work."

The constable shook his head. "There wasn't much I could do at that point except collect pieces of the puzzle and try to keep an open mind. So when I went back there tonight, I truly meant only to learn if he'd seen Betty today. Toby covers more ground than most people, including the woods and orchards and out-of-the-way places between the

Glengarry place and the schoolhouse. But he wasn't there."

"How do you know he's really gone?" my mother asked.

"Well, I suppose I don't. But he wasn't in the shack. No fire. Cold coals. No guns. No camera. No nothing." He heaved a sigh. Looked at me and away.

"He had stuck pictures all over the walls," he said. "I had my searchlight in my truck. Spent some time in there, looking at those pictures. I tried to pull one off, but he used pine sap and it was on there good."

He took a crumpled photograph from his pocket and handed it to my father, who smoothed it out and looked at it for a moment before passing it to my mother.

"So?"

"So you don't think it's odd that a man like Toby is sneaking around taking pictures of your daughter when she's unaware?"

I moved around behind my mother and peered over her shoulder. The picture showed me walking down the path to school. Sunlight coming through the branches lit up my face, but the rest of me looked vague in the shadows. It felt strange, seeing what I looked like when I thought I was alone. I had never known that Toby was there, in the trees nearby, watching.

"It's odd the way Toby is odd," my mother said. "But that doesn't mean it's something worse."

Aunt Lily stood up suddenly. "More of his pictures came back in today's mail," she said, and hurried off to her room.

When she returned, I reached out my hand. "He wanted me to give them to him as soon as they came back," I said.

"Well, you can't very well do that when he's run off," she said, handing the package to the constable.

He opened it, took the pictures out of the envelope inside, and held them well away from his wet coat as he looked at each one. His face became tougher as he did.

He held one back, passing the rest to my parents, who looked at them together, Aunt Lily across the table fidgeting impatiently.

"What?" she said. "Pass those here."

"Some yellow trees," my father said. "A field of pumpkins." He paused and turned to the constable. "But I suspect that one you've got there is something different."

The constable nodded. He passed it over, and I moved behind my father so I could see it.

We were looking at the schoolhouse road from high above. Some tree branches split the scene, but I could make out Mr. Ansel's grays, his wagon filled with apples. Ruth, lying in the road. Mr. Ansel climbing down from his wagon. And me.

"Oh my Lord," my mother said quietly.

"But this doesn't mean anything," I said. "Just because he took that picture doesn't mean he threw the rock."

"I'm afraid it means quite a lot, young lady," the constable said. "Especially since Betty is missing and Toby's gone, after she accused him of hurting Ruth, after I went down there and told him so—and you must realize that he knew we'd be looking at these very pictures at some point—all of which adds up to a worrisome conclusion. But right now the most important thing is finding Betty."

"And that terrible man," Aunt Lily said. She should have looked harmless, in her robe and rollers, but she didn't.

The constable turned to me. "Mrs. Taylor told me Andy was at the schoolhouse today, looking for Betty. Do you know anything about that, Annabelle?"

I shrugged. "Andy and Betty really like each other." I thought about it for a moment. "They usually disappear at recess. You already know about the belfry. And I think she and Andy sharpened up a wire and strung it across the path. It cut my little brother across the forehead." I traced a line across my own.

The constable shook his head. "Another story I need to hear. But right now I'm going to talk to Andy. Depending on what he has to say, we'll round up some people and go looking. I hope you can help with that, John."

"And what about Toby?" Aunt Lily demanded. "I certainly don't like the idea of a crazy man running loose around here." She tightened her robe across her chest.

"I suspect he's long gone," the constable said. "Probably miles from here by now. But I'll let the state barracks know the situation in case he shows up somewhere else."

He climbed to his feet. "In the meantime, finding Betty should be our only purpose." He gave Aunt Lily a stern look. "Nothing else."

She lifted her chin. "And when she's found?"

"I promise I'll look into this," he said, tucking the picture in his pocket, "but leave it to me now."

He turned back to my father. "Are those dogs of yours any good at tracking?"

"Not much, unless there's a meat loaf on the run," my father said.

"Well, you might want to take them along, just in case. But first, Andy. Let me hear what he's got to say."

CHAPTER THIRTEEN

It wasn't easy to get back to sleep that night.

I'd been over to Andy's farm with my father many times to trade produce for dairy—apples for cheese, beans for butter—so I couldn't help but picture it now, dark and quiet, then the constable knocking on the door, the porch light coming on, Andy's father appearing, rumpled with sleep. Rousing Andy to come down for questions.

I hoped Andy knew where Betty was. Maybe she had realized that all her lies were about to catch up with her and she had run away. Or maybe she'd gone out exploring, though probably not in the rain, probably not without Andy.

I couldn't imagine that Toby had anything to do with it. In a way, I wished he was, indeed, far from here by now.

But the bigger part of me hoped he'd turn up as always.

Had he left the camera hanging from a hook in his shack, I would have believed him gone. Toby would not have taken our camera, though it was really his, too.

When I finally wore myself out with thinking, I dreamed about Betty, but nothing clear or memorable. Just a murky swirl that faded as soon as I woke.

It wasn't morning. Too dark for morning, but something more. The feel of night. Still, I could sense movement below.

This time, when I went downstairs, I found that my parents were up and dressed, breakfast on the table, though it was just four o'clock, early even for farmers at this time of year. Constable Oleska sat at the table, eating eggs and sausage.

"Did you find her?" I asked from the doorway, blinking in the light.

"Annabelle, what are you doing up?" my mother said. "It's still nighttime. Go on back to bed."

"I'm all slept out," I said. "Did Betty come home, Constable?"

"No, I'm afraid not," he said. "We'll start the search at first light. Her grandpa and some neighbors are already out there, but they won't find anything in the dark. The rest of us will head out soon, fresh and dry, and we'll find her if she's to be found."

He didn't look fresh and dry to me. I suspected he'd been up all night. "What did Andy say?"

"Your parents and I were just getting into that," the constable said. He talked while he ate, obviously famished. "Andy's a little too big for his britches, so I expected some lip, but he was shook up pretty good. He told me that he and Betty had planned to skip school and spend the day together, tramping around the farms and, as he put it, 'having a lark.'"

The constable shook his head. "The boy was mostly calf when he talked about Betty. All the rough gone out of him. He said they were supposed to meet at the Turtle Stone first thing yesterday morning, but at the last minute his pa made him stay home to fix a fence. By the time he got to the stone, she was gone. He went looking for her, wound up at school, found out she hadn't shown up, so he went to the Glengarrys'. Nobody was there. He figured they'd taken Betty someplace. So he went home."

"Did you ask him about the belfry and all that?" I asked.

"Not now, Annabelle," my mother said. "There will be time for that business when she's found."

Which made sense, I suppose, but I didn't see this as separate strands. It was, to my thinking, a rope, any part of which was twined with every other part. But I held my peace.

My mother warmed the constable's coffee and the three of them talked about the search while I helped myself to breakfast and listened.

And then Aunt Lily appeared in the doorway. She'd taken the rollers from her hair and it fell in anemic curls around her shoulders. She was still in her robe and slippers, traces of night cream under her eyes. "Did you find him?" she asked.

"Who?" we all said, like a family of owls.

"Toby," she snapped.

"I'm not looking for Toby," the constable said. "I thought you meant Andy."

"Who isn't lost and doesn't need finding," she said. She poured herself a cup of coffee and sat at the table. "It's Toby you ought to be looking for before he snatches another young girl."

"Lily!" my mother said sharply.

"You think Annabelle shouldn't hear such things? I agree, Sarah, but you're the one who thinks she belongs here at the table with adults. And I'd like to know, Constable: Has it occurred to you that the two of them are together somewhere, Betty his prisoner?"

The constable sighed. "Of course it occurred to me, Lily," he said, "and I've already called the state police so they can start looking for him. Or them."

Such talk shocked me deeply. I had never thought such

a thing. I was beginning to agree with my aunt about one thing, at least.

"I think I will go back to bed," I said.

My mother gave me a sad little smile. "Good girl," she said. "And maybe you and the boys should stay home from school today. You're tired. And nobody will be paying much attention to their schoolwork with all this going on."

Another shock, since my mother had never suggested such a thing before. We had to be pretty sick or there had to be a blizzard raging to keep us away from our lessons.

I nodded. "Okay."

I tried to go back to sleep. I really did. But I could not stop thinking about what my aunt Lily had said. I couldn't imagine why Toby would want to take Betty with him, make her his "prisoner." She was a nasty girl, and he knew it. But for some reason Aunt Lily and even the constable thought they might be together.

I was sure they were wrong.

And I feared that I was the only one who cared as much about helping Toby as finding Betty.

My parents liked him, true enough, but a missing girl was a missing girl. Nobody else was likely to put Toby ahead of that.

I lay in my bed and tried to admit that Toby had left our hills. But to have taken the camera? To have left without saying good-bye? Without even some small remembrance to let us know . . . to let *me* know that he was sorry to be leaving?

I could not believe that. I was convinced that Toby had not left after all. That he was right where he was supposed to be. Right where the police would be able to find him as soon as they went looking.

And I asked myself, in the face of this possibility, what I was prepared to do about it.

I dressed in the dark, adding layers so I could stay out long in the cold, and crept down the stairs. When I peeked into the kitchen, I found that my father and Constable Oleska were gone. My mother worked at the sink, her back to me. No sign of Aunt Lily.

I crept into the mudroom, aptly named given the amount of slop we'd all tracked in over the past day, carried my boots to the door, pulled them on from the threshold before I stepped into the wet, and quietly closed the door behind me.

Anyone who's ever gone from warm and bright to cold and dark knows how I felt. To my back, all safe things. Before me, a night not as black as it had appeared through the windows, but dark enough, the sky overhead clear now, no clouds to whiten the darkness, precious little starlight and no moon at all. The trees bowed to one another as if before a dance, making their own sad music. And I was suddenly filled with misgivings.

I had been out in the night before, many times, but never alone, not past the end of our lane.

Still, as I hesitated, my eyes adjusted to the night and the darkness paled some. And it would be morning soon. And I knew where I was going.

Toby's shack was in Cobb Hollow below the Glengarry place, on the other side of our hill from Wolf Hollow, away from the schoolhouse, set in the woods not far off a dirt lane I'd walked many times. It wasn't too far. And there wasn't much between here and there except woods.

I didn't like the thought of bears, but I'd seen one only once, and it had scampered away at the sight of me. Sometimes people talked about a mountain lion in the area, but not for a long time. No more wolves around here. And I really wasn't completely alone. With me, out here in the dark, were men searching for Betty.

I would have to be careful to stay out of their way. If they mistook me for her, it would deal everyone a terrible disappointment. And me some trouble.

So I kept to the woods, following deer trails, careful in the slick leaves. I knew my way simply by heading downhill. It was difficult to get lost in these hills since every hollow had a lane or a proper road running through it and, alongside, a house now and then, each one of which I knew.

When I reached level ground, I took the dirt road toward Silas Cobb's old place. I didn't see a soul, but once or twice I heard people calling back and forth in the distance. The burned-out foundation of the Cobb house was set back in the trees far enough so it was not visible from the road, but there was still a passable lane and a crooked wooden post sign that said COBB to mark the place.

The lane was marshy, and the trees on either side bent low overhead, making a tunnel that dripped and trembled in the wind. There was no sign of a clearing where the Cobb house had once stood. It had been entirely swallowed up in bramble, off to one side of the lane, and trees had grown up through the foundation, but they were thin enough that some sky showed above, and I could tell from the suggestion of blue in the black that the sun would soon be up.

As I paused there, I heard something new.

It wasn't wind. Nor was it the sound of searchers in the distance. More like an animal sound. A call of some kind, I thought. Not owl. Not fox.

Most ground animals and brooding birds kept quiet at night, for fear of attracting the attention of predators, so whatever was making that odd noise had no such fear.

I'd heard a porcupine once or twice. A blend of tooth-chatter and whine, mixed with the mild bleat of a bike horn with a leaky bulb.

This sound was something like that, and I was suddenly frightened. I'd seen a dog once, its nose bristling with quills, and I had no intention of tangling with a porcupine.

But as I stood there the sound stopped. I listened for it, but all I heard was wind.

Toby's shack was just another bit ahead, behind a stand of thick trees and ivy. He had kept the area around it clear. I could make out a stump with an ax in it and I thought, unbidden, of King Arthur pulling Excalibur from the stone.

At the door to the shack, I hesitated for only a moment, the word *prisoner* rising in my mind, before knocking.

To my astonishment, something inside moved. Made noise.

I stepped back away from the door just as it opened.

And there was Toby.

CHAPTER FOURTEEN

Toby was wrapped in an army blanket, his feet bare.

"Annabelle." It was both statement and question.

"Hey, Toby." I realized that I had no idea what his last name was. No way to call him Mister anything.

He looked past me, perhaps expecting my father to walk out of the gloom. "What's wrong?"

"The constable told us you'd gone away and might have taken Betty with you or that you know where she is. And he called the state police and they are going to be here soon to look for you." I had more to say, but that much had used up all my breath.

He thought about that for a minute. "The girl who said I threw a rock at the German."

I nodded, the beginnings of confusion like an itch

inside my head. "Yes. She's been missing since yesterday morning. Didn't you know that? People are looking for her everywhere." I could see that this was truly news to him. "The constable came to see you last night, but you weren't here. He thought you'd left. Maybe with Betty?" My voice trailed away. His white face was even whiter now.

"You didn't know she was missing?"

He shook his head. "I was fishing under the creek bridge. Traded the fish to Turner for jerky."

The Turners raised cattle and pigs for meat. My father liked their jerky, too, and it lasted for a long time, with or without an icebox.

"Stayed in their barn until the rain let up. Came back here late." He turned and looked into the smokehouse. "Someone stole one of my pictures."

I'd never heard Toby say so much at one time.

"Constable Oleska took it," I said. "The one that showed me on the path to school. And he looked at the pictures that just came back in the mail, too. I'm sorry about that, but Aunt Lily gave them to him. You took one from up the hill, above Mr. Ansel's wagon, the day Ruth got hurt."

Toby gave me a hard look.

"I didn't throw that rock," he said.

Hearing him say it was good, though I hadn't realized I needed to hear it until I did.

"I believe you," I said. "But now they know you were on that hill, and Betty said she saw you throw the rock and now she's missing. They think you did some bad things, Toby."

Toby took a long breath. "I did," he said.

I crossed my arms over my chest, which made me feel bigger. "What did you do?"

He pulled the blanket tighter around himself.

I waited.

I said, "But you didn't throw that rock." It still sounded too much like a question.

He shook his head. "She did."

I was surprised, though I had suspected as much.

"You saw her?"

"I tried to take her picture, but she threw it so fast. And then she ducked into the bushes. And that boy with her. But not before she saw me a bit higher up than they were. And knew that I'd seen her."

"Then why didn't you say so when my father came to talk with you?"

Toby looked away. "Things come out right. Or they don't."

"What? Toby, you should have told him what happened. Nobody's going to believe you now."

"Nothing I can do about that," he said.

An odd and frustrating way to look at the world, but I was not Toby, and he was not me.

We stood for a long moment. All around us, birds woke up the sky.

And I heard, in the distance, people calling for Betty.

Toby took a step back into the smokehouse. Which made up my mind for me.

"All right," I said firmly. "I want you to come with me now."

Toby's mouth twitched just a little. It was the closest thing to a smile that I'd ever seen on him. "You sound like your mother."

I took that as a compliment. "Good. Because if she were here she'd say the same thing. Please, now," I said, "will you get dressed and come along?"

Toby seemed to be torn. "Where to?"

"Somewhere safe until we can sort things out."

He shook his head. "Doesn't matter much to me."

"Well, it matters to me," I said. "And if you don't care one way or the other, how about we do it my way?"

Again, that twitch.

Again, in the distance, the sound of people calling.

After a few minutes, Toby joined me outside the smokehouse. He was dressed as always, the camera around his neck, his guns slung across his back.

The walk back up the hill was harder, but Toby climbed behind me, waiting while I tree-pulled myself up the steepest parts, worse because they were slippery. The strengthening light helped a lot, but it worried me, too.

We were very watchful and as quiet as we could be, given the shouting in the distance. Had I feared real hunters, I would have worn red, but we were both in brown and black, invisible if we stood still and hid our faces.

As we crested the hill and made our way toward home, I realized that anyone would be able to see us through the farmhouse windows if we came across our pasture, so we kept to the woods until we were on the far side of our barn, cut across the open quickly, and ducked in from the back. I went ahead first, calling to see if anyone was around, happy that the dogs were part of the search, pretending to help.

When one of the horses swung his big head over his stable door and looked at me curiously, I nearly jumped out of my skin.

"Time for you to be out, Bill," I said, unlatching the Dutch door and pulling it open. He snorted at me and sauntered down the aisle toward the big open gate that led to the pasture. I freed Dinah next, and she followed him into the sunlight, her tail twitching. Next, the milk cows, Molly and Daisy. We never named the calves, since we had to give them up so quickly, but our milk cows we kept until they had to go.

I put out my hand as they lumbered past me, and the second of them planted her big square black nose in my palm for a moment, the hair on it a soft bristle.

Had my father not been out searching for Betty, he would already have set them loose by now. I hoped that the sight of them in the pasture would keep anyone from coming out to the barn to do that chore, though they might come to see who had done it.

I wondered if anyone had missed me yet.

"Follow me," I whisper-called to Toby, opening the door to the stairs that ran up the middle of the barn to the threshing floor.

Ours was a banked barn set into the side of a hill with stalls down below that opened onto a long aisle. A cistern squatted on a slab at the back of the barn, next to a long corncrib.

A huge pair of side doors on the top level opened to a lane and staging area on the upper slope. We could drive hay wagons up that lane and in through the side of the barn, store the big equipment in winter, work there in foul weather. Big tubs of oats stood next to grain chutes that led straight down to mangers in the stalls below. Part of this upper level had a very high, peaked roof hung with ropes and tackle for hoisting bales into the loft that consumed the better part of the space along the rafters.

It was an old barn with some missing planks and years of dirt and straw built up on the floor, but it was dry enough and plenty snug in the hayloft, where my father liked to nap on rainy days. I hoped for a nice stretch of dry weather.

At the foot of the long ladder to the loft, Toby stopped. He looked at the ladder, looked at me, looked back at the ladder. I started up. "Come on," I said over my shoulder. "You can wait in the loft until everything gets sorted out."

But he stayed where he was. "I don't like high places," he said.

I almost fell off the ladder. He didn't look pleased when I started to laugh, so I stopped and climbed back down.

Here was a big man in a black oilcloth coat, three guns slung across his back, long gnarled hair and beard, a black hat, a white face barely visible in the shadow of its rim. A man who'd been through a terrible war. A man who lived mostly on game and berries in a smokehouse in the woods.

"You're afraid to climb up to the loft?" I asked him.

He ducked his head. Shifted his guns.

I chewed my lip. "You live in hill country," I said. "You're high up most of the time."

He shook his head. "Not the same."

"Well," I said. "You can either climb up to that hayloft or you can hide in the corncrib with the mice." This time, I, too, heard my mother in my voice.

Perhaps it was the word *hide* or the idea of clambering into a corncrib that did it. Perhaps the suggestion that he was a mouse. Toby didn't say. But after a moment he flapped a hand at me and, when I began again to climb the ladder, followed.

From the top, I looked back and saw him slowly climbing, two feet on every rung, gripping the side rails hard, his left hand knotty and slick with scars, focused on what he was doing, never looking down. The hardest part was at the top. He slapped his good hand out flat on the floor of the loft and dug his nails in. I grabbed his wrist, though largely for moral support, and he crawled off the ladder and clear of the edge of the loft, breathing harder than he had as we climbed the hill out of Cobb Hollow. I didn't tell him that it would be harder still to climb down.

At least I could assume he'd stay where he was for a while. That first step down onto the ladder from above would keep him put while I figured out what to do next.

"I'll be back as soon as I can with some food and water," I said. "And a bucket for, well, you know." I could feel myself pink up. "If anybody comes in the barn, just scoot back between the bales and stay quiet. The boys might come around, but they'll probably stay out of the loft."

Toby sat down on a bale of hay. When he laid his guns aside and took off his hat, he looked like a boy himself. Much older, of course, but just as young.

"Don't worry," I said. "Everything will be fine."

CHAPTER FIFTEEN

Before I returned to the house, I wandered around outside the pasture fence, picking milkweed pods until my pockets bulged with them.

"Where have you been, Annabelle?" my mother said when I came through the mudroom door. "One girl gone is one too many. Do you know how worried I was when I found your bed empty?"

I didn't want to lie to my mother, so I aimed for as much truth as I could. "You were in the cellar when I got up," I said. "The horses and cows needed to be put to pasture, so I did that, and then I figured I'd gather some milkweed for the troops." I pulled a soggy pod from my pocket. "But I didn't have a bag with me."

There wasn't much we children could do to assist the war effort, but we'd been asked to collect milkweed pods for their floss, which floated better than cork. The navy needed it for life jackets, so all across the country children had been put on milkweed detail. "I'll take the boys out and collect the rest before it's too late."

Here was something a farmer dreaded: milkweed seeds wafting across orchards, setting down roots where they'd make a nuisance of themselves, driving the livestock mad if they rooted in pastures.

My mother looked askance at me. "How come you're wearing so many clothes but no coat?"

I shrugged. "I don't know."

Which, oddly, seemed to satisfy her.

"Well, until everything's calmed down around here you let me know before you go someplace."

"Where is everybody?"

"Your brothers were up with the sun and pestered your father until he let them go on the search." She sighed. "I can just see it. Your father, two boys, four dogs. Your poor grandfather driving the truck around in circles, looking for some way to be useful."

Which was fine with me, as long as they all stayed away from the barn.

While my mother returned to her chores, I helped myself to some rolls from the bread box, filled a mug with coffee from a pot on the stove, and headed for the cellar.

It was a big cellar with stone walls and floors and four rooms. One was for laundry, perpetually damp but clean, the wringer washer in one corner, lines strung from wall to wall, a wicker basket on a long table, in it a cloth sack of wooden pins, tin buckets for hauling wash water from the well, a one-burner stove for heating the water, and a drain in the floor.

In another room, shelves lined with newspaper held jars of jam, pickles, peppers, beans, tomatoes, peaches, peas, and corn.

The coal room had a chute set up close to the ceiling so my father could shovel the coal in from the lane above. It was a filthy, sooty place where nobody went until winter came and the furnace wanted to be fed.

The fourth room was for everything else that didn't belong above stairs. Buckets that needed to be patched. Empty canning jars. Gardening tools. Bulbs dug up and stored in bushels of peat.

There was a door leading from the back of the cellar to the outside, lower on the hill than the rest of the house. Just outside was a separate entrance to the root cellar where we stored potatoes, onions, beets, carrots: anything that needed to last as long into the winter as possible.

I took a tin bucket that was still sound but had seen better days and filled it with provisions: the rolls, a pot of strawberry jam, some carrots, a couple of empty Mason jars and lids; I filled one with the mug of coffee. The others I would fill at the barn cistern.

I left the bucket outside the cellar door and climbed the stairs.

I found my mother stripping the sheets from my grandparents' bed while my grandmother sat in her rocker, darning a sock.

"I'm going back for more milkweed," I said.

And that's when I felt the first wave of sorrow that came from keeping a new secret. Perhaps, by the end of this day, Betty would be found and Toby could return to his smokehouse, no harm done.

If not, I would tell my mother. I could not keep this secret forever. Nor could I hide Toby for long, cloistered in the hayloft like a stray cat.

"Don't forget to take a bag this time," my mother said as she stuffed the soiled linens in a pillowcase.

"I won't." I watched the two of them at their work for another moment. So different. So much the same. The room filled with things they'd made. All of it worn to softness.

The second wave of sorrow, now, was for Toby, too long deprived of such things, if he'd ever had them at all.

Without school, without brothers underfoot, I had plenty of time to myself. I would have spent much of it in the barn anyway, with a book and rock doves for company, but today was Toby's.

"It's just me," I whisper-called at the foot of the ladder. No answer.

I climbed carefully, the bucket heavy, the metal bail hurting my fingers a little. When I reached the top, I set the bucket aside and climbed clear of the ladder. "Toby?"

He appeared then from behind a wall of bales. He'd taken off his coat. Without it, he was as thin as a spring bear. Hatless, he had no shadow in which to hide. His eyes were blue.

"You made yourself a hideaway," I said. "That was smart." I gestured at the bucket. "Are you hungry?"

He shrugged. "I have jerky."

"And now you have bread and jam, carrots, and well water. Coffee, though it will be cold if you don't drink it now. I can bring you more after supper."

Toby still hadn't stepped any closer to where I stood by the edge of the loft. A rail ran along there, but no spindles. Next to nothing, for a man afraid of heights.

"I'll bring more water, too, but there's a cistern with a hand pump where we came into the barn. If you need to wash up, after it gets dark. Or you could go a little farther down the pasture. There's a trough. A spring feeds it so it's nice, fresh water. Cold, though."

I imagined that Toby normally bathed and washed his clothes in the creek that ran near his smokehouse, though his coat was so stiff with weather and soot that he never seemed particularly clean, regardless. Now, as he stood there without it, he looked almost respectable, though his hair and beard were long and tangled. "But if you don't want to climb down . . ."

I moved the bucket well away from the edge of the loft, next to a bale Toby could use for a seat. He came closer, and I was reminded of the stray dogs when they first arrived at the farm.

"Nuts," I said. "I forgot a knife for the jam."

From his pocket, Toby pulled a jackknife.

He sat on a bale and cut a roll in half. Twisted the band off the jam jar, pried off the lid with the tip of his knife, and spread some jam on half the roll. He held it out to me.

"Toby, that's for you. I can eat at the house."

He held out the half until I took it.

Toby spread his portion with jam and set it on his knee while he wiped the knife clean between his fingers, closed it, put it away. He opened the jar of coffee.

"I'm sorry if it's cold," I said.

He ate the roll thoughtfully, drinking from the jar.

I took a bite and only then realized how hungry I was. It seemed years since I had awoken to find the constable at our table and the state police on their way.

We ate in silence. Toby finished the coffee.

"Do you want me to bring you a book to read?" I asked, fearing, as I said it, that he might not know how.

Toby looked at me sharply.

"We have lots of books. All kinds. My brothers like Robert Louis Stevenson. I do, too." I shrugged. "If you want, I could bring you something. But you'll have to read it while there's daylight."

Toby didn't need to think about it. "Whatever you have," he said.

I sat down on the floor and crossed my legs. Tried to decide if it would be right to ask him some questions.

I twirled a stem of hay between my palms. "Can I ask you a question, Toby?"

He laced his fingers. "You just did."

I saw his mouth twitch again with the seed of a smile.

I almost said, "Can I ask you another question?" but realized that that would itself be another question. So I said, "What's your name? Your family name?"

But Toby didn't answer. He looked away. "No," I said quickly. "I have a better one." I wanted to know where he was from, if he had any brothers or sisters, whether he'd ever had a dog and what he'd called it, how old he'd been when he went to fight in the war, how he'd come to be hurt, how old he was now (though my mother always said he had to be forty-four, forty-five or so), and what he'd meant when he said that he'd done "something bad."

"What's your favorite food?" I blurted, feeling like a child.

This time, Toby looked straight at me and, after a brief pause, said, "Hickory nut pie."

"Really? My mother makes really good hickory nut pie. Did you know that?"

He nodded. "She once saved me a piece. Best thing I ever ate."

Toby's voice sounded different. Softer. "Said she was sorry it didn't have any cream on top." He shook his head. "I don't know what I would have done if it had been any better than it was. Died, maybe."

We spent some time like that, me asking small questions, Toby giving me longer and longer answers, until we were simply talking, Toby asking me questions, too. So I told him about my grandmother, whom he had seldom seen. And about Aunt Lily, though all I said was, "And then there's my aunt Lily, who's a postmistress," at which Toby interjected a quick "Yes, I've seen her," and nothing more.

Until we got to the point when I had to ask him something harder, though I felt it was mine to ask. "What did you mean when you told my father that they'd made scratches on the Turtle Stone?"

Toby pulled back a little, tightened up to where he'd been, and spent a moment in thought. "They were sharpening a wire."

"Betty and Andy."

He nodded.

"Do you know what they did with it?"

He nodded again. "If I'd seen them put it there, I would have taken it before it cut your brother."

"You heard about that?"

"I saw you three coming out of Wolf Hollow, James bleeding, that girl, Betty, watching you cross the field. When you were gone, I went down the path and saw her unwinding the wire from one of the trees. She ran off when she saw me coming."

"The wire was gone when I took my father to show him."

"She took it with her." He looked straight at me. "She was a bad girl."

I didn't know what to think about the "was."

I stood up and dusted off my seat. "I have to go gather up some milkweed," I said.

"Why?"

"The navy needs it for life jackets."

Toby didn't say another word.

"I'll bring you a book later," I said. And left him to himself.

CHAPTER SIXTEEN

Now I actually had to fill a sack with milkweed pods, which took longer than I liked. But I reminded myself that while Toby might need me, so did the troops. I pictured a boy lost in a stormy sea, his life jacket keeping him above water until he could be rescued. A life jacket filled with milkweed floss from our farm, perhaps from the sack over my shoulder.

I picked until my fingers were sore and the sack overflowing.

Alongside the grassy lane between the barn and the house, there was a wagon shed where I spread the pods on a workbench to dry. Said hello to the cats napping in the wagon bed. And went on to my regular chores, long overdue on this very odd day.

First, I gathered eggs from the chicken coop, a nice place in cool weather, awful in the heat. Our birds were accustomed to me and didn't raise a fuss, even when I reached underneath them to take their warm eggs, leaving some with the brood hens so we would always have young birds coming of age to replace those we ate.

Of all my chores, the worst was plucking a chicken after my mother had wrung its neck and dunked it in boiling water.

For the dozen eggs in my basket, I thanked the birds with corn and dried marigolds and left them in peace.

At the well by the house, which had a proper housing so it was safe and neat enough for my mother's liking, I washed the eggs under the pump and carried them inside.

"Good girl," my grandmother said after I took off my boots and put the eggs in a bowl by the stove.

I went up to my room and stripped off some of the layers I'd worn for early-morning warmth, changed my damp socks for dry ones, and ran a brush through my hair.

Back in the kitchen, I helped my mother and grandmother with a huge pot of soup. We had no idea when the searchers would return or how many would come back with my father for a hot meal, so we browned onions and stewing beef, added vegetables and tomato juice my mother had put up in August, and left the pot to simmer.

My mother checked my hands to make sure they were clean enough, and then she set a huge bowl on the kitchen table, took off the damp linen that covered it, and let me punch down the dough that had risen into a soft, white belly. We all three twisted off dollops to shape into rolls, lined them up on greased pans, and slid them into the oven.

In no time, the kitchen was so fragrant with soup at the simmer and browning rolls that I was hungry all over again. I could only imagine how Toby must have felt.

"Go on now, and redd up your room, Annabelle," my mother said.

Which I did in a trice, making my bed and putting away the clothes I'd shed. On second thought, I pulled the case from my pillow and spread the quilt over it again. Then I went hunting.

From the room where my brothers slept, I took *Treasure Island*, which my grandmother had just read to them for the third time and wouldn't be wanting again for a long while. I put it in the pillowcase.

From my parents' room I took an old pair of my father's pants, a soft flannel shirt much like every other one he owned, some thick socks, and a pair of skivvies. In the past, my mother had given identical ones to Toby, so these were perfect. From my mother's sewing kit, I borrowed her sharpest scissors.

All of this went into the pillowcase, along with a bar of Lava soap and a clean towel from the washroom.

At every turn, I was but steps from my mother or grandmother, but they were busy, and I was soft-footed as I took the pillowcase down to the cellar and left it just outside the door, behind a bush.

When I returned to the kitchen, I found my mother making pies.

"I want to search, too," I said.

She turned from her work, hands white with flour. "Oh, Annabelle, I don't think that's a good idea. But when your father comes back with the boys you can ask him. I expect your brothers will be happy to stay home after a morning tramping through wet woods. Maybe you can take their place."

All I'd really wanted was a reason to take a jar of soup and some rolls and head back out again, and now here I might have talked myself into an afternoon searching for a girl who had made a mess of things for everyone.

"All right," I said slowly. "But no one's looking right around here. Why don't I go on a little walk through the woods back of the barn? I could take my lunch with me. I won't go far."

My mother considered me for a long moment. "Do you know more about this than you're telling me, Annabelle?"

I forced myself to hold her gaze. "More about what?"

"About Betty gone missing." By now she had turned fully toward me, her floury hands poised in the air as if she were about to lead a choir.

The truth suited, though it was a lie, too, and once again I knew that I would not be able to keep my secret for much longer.

"Nope," I said. "I have no idea where she is. But I'd like to help find her."

My mother nodded thoughtfully. "All right. Take what you want and go on out, but not off our hill, do you understand?"

"Yes, ma'am," I said.

I chose a coat with deep pockets. In one I put a Mason jar filled with hot soup, wrapped in a dishcloth, and a spoon. In the other, a hot roll with a coin of butter tucked inside, the hole pinched shut, wrapped in a sheet of waxed paper.

"You look like you've got jodhpurs on," my mother said as I stood by the door, ready to go.

"What are jodhpurs?" I said.

"Never mind. Just watch yourself, Annabelle, and don't go too far. When you hear the dinner bell, you'll know your father's back."

"Yes, ma'am," I said again.

"And take that egg basket back out to the coop," she said.

"Yes, ma'am."

Which was one "Yes, ma'am" too many.

My mother bent a little to look straight into my face. "What are you not telling me?" she said, not angry but plenty serious.

I looked steadily back at her. "I'm afraid," I said.

I didn't know where that came from. It just came. And it was the truth.

She straightened up. "Of what?"

I shrugged. "Everything. Betty. Betty missing. Toby missing. What Aunt Lily said about Toby taking Betty prisoner. The police coming here. I've never even seen a policeman."

And then I was crying.

I was crying, and I was more surprised about it than my mother, who bent down again and put her arms around me and made soft noises in my ear.

"It's all right, Annabelle. It's all right. Everything will be all right."

Which was what I had said to Toby, whether I believed it or not.

I hoped my mother believed it.

But I had learned, over the past weeks, that believing in something doesn't always make it so.

I wiped my eyes and put on my cap. "I don't know what

that was all about," I said. "I'm not really very scared. I just wish they would find Betty so things could get back to normal."

My mother smiled at me. "Me, too. Now go on and have a look around, but remember what I said about staying close by."

When she turned back to her work, I said, "What would you say if I asked you to make a hickory nut pie?"

We had a few hickory trees and harvested enough for our own use, but the nuts were dear and generally meant for holidays.

She picked up her rolling pin. "I would say that you might expect something of the kind before long."

"Don't forget to ring the bell when they get back," I said.

I went out the door, down and around the back of the house, fetched the pillowcase, and swung it over one shoulder. Feeling a little like a hobo, I headed down farther into the trees and across the side of the wooded hill below the barn until I had worked my way around the back of it and could enter, again, unseen from the house or the lane.

The horses watched me cross the pasture, ready for an apple if I had one, but I paid them no mind, and after a moment they returned to their grazing.

"Me, again," I called as I climbed the ladder to the hayloft.

This time, Toby had come out of his hiding place to meet me. "I didn't expect you back so soon," he said.

"I brought some more food. When everybody comes in from searching I'll have to go back, and I may not be out here again for a while." I emptied my pockets of the soup and bread. Handed Toby the spoon. "Lunch," I said.

Watching Toby eat that soup and bread was a little like watching somebody pray. He made it last, dipping the spoon slowly into the Mason jar and then, toward the end, tipping the dregs into his mouth. When he bit into the roll and found the surprise of soft butter inside, he laughed. Just one quick burst.

He seemed as startled by that as I was. I'd not heard him laugh before. Nor seen him smile.

He finished the roll, capped the jar, and set it aside. "Thank you," he said.

"You're welcome."

He gestured at the pillowcase. "What have you got there?"

I knelt and opened it, pulling out the book. "Well, this is *Treasure Island*." I held it out.

The book was soft from handling, its corners stubbed, but Toby wiped his hands carefully on his pant legs before he reached for it.

"Thank you," he said.

"You're welcome," I replied. "There's a big hatch behind those bales, for lowering them out to the pasture. You can open one of the shutters and get some light to read by."

Toby nodded.

"Can I ask you something?" I said.

He raised his eyebrows. "You just did."

I smiled and popped a fist against my forehead. "Okay." And here I paused, suddenly afraid. "I like your hair and all. I like it very much. It's very nice hair."

"Thank you," he said again, puzzled. "Is that a question?"

"I used to have long hair like that, but I hated when I got rats in it and my mother would about snap my neck trying to comb it out."

He waited.

"And then my aunt Lily cut it short one morning when I came in from chores with chicken feathers in my braids. My mother about had a seizure, but in the end she liked it better. Said I looked like Amelia Earhart."

Toby nodded. "You do, a little."

"And I wondered if you might let me give you a trim? I brought some scissors, just in case. But I like your hair very much, Toby. It's nice hair." I felt like an idiot.

Toby pulled a hank around and looked at how long it was. "Keeps me warm in winter," he said.

I nodded. "I'll knit you a scarf instead."

I would have to learn to knit first, but he didn't know that.

"Why?"

"Why should you cut your hair?"

He nodded.

"Same reason I think you should trim your beard," I said. "So you'll feel tidy. I like to feel tidy. I like how light I feel." I shook my head. "Nothing to get in my eyes. Tidy."

Which was the truth. What I didn't say was that his hair and his beard hid him too much, as if he were peeking out from somewhere inside himself.

"And then," I added, before I lost my nerve, "you can have a good wash under the pump and put on some fresh things." I pulled the soap and towel and clothes out of the pillowcase and set them on a bale of hay.

I stood back and waited.

"Am I too dirty?" he asked. He held out his hands in front of him. It hurt me to look at the scarred one, how it was puckered and gnarled.

"No, not at all. Aw, I'm sorry, Toby," I said. "I don't mean that at all. Just that it will feel good to be, well . . ."

"Tidy," he said.

"Yes," I said. "Tidy."

I thought that if I said the word *tidy* one more time he

would pick me up and pitch me out of the loft.

But after a bit he nodded and said, "If you think so."

We started with the hair. First, I cut off most of it in big hunks and put them in a pile to bury in the woods later. With the worst of it gone, I set to making it even. Tidy. Which I was ill equipped to do. But I'd watched my mother trim up my brothers and knew essentially how it should be done. I was glad, though, that I hadn't brought a mirror.

When I was finished, Toby looked astonishingly unlike Toby.

"You look like your own brother," I said, meaning a version of himself.

Toby looked at me quite seriously. "I don't have a brother."

"Sister?"

He shook his head.

I paused. Bit back my curiosity.

"Now the beard," I said.

Toby jerked his head back. "Not too short," he said.

I nodded. "Don't worry."

But before I could begin, I heard the dinner bell ringing hard back at the house.

"Uh-oh," I said, handing him the scissors. "My father's home. You'll have to do the beard yourself."

He stood up suddenly. "Will you let me know if they found her?"

"I will," I said. "But be careful now." I returned the soup jar and spoon to my pocket. "I don't know who might come out here next. Hide all the rest of this behind the bales, okay? I'll be back as soon as I can."

This time, when I looked back up from the threshing floor, Toby was peering over the loft rail.

If I hadn't known it was him, I wouldn't have recognized Toby looking down at me. He was that different, shorn.

CHAPTER SEVENTEEN

I expected to find my grandfather and my father and my brothers, maybe some hungry neighbors come home for soup.

These I got, but much more, too.

The yard around the mudroom door was littered with dogs of all colors and sizes, empty feed bowls, water bowls ringed by tongue-splash.

Inside, the mudroom had earned its name, hemmed with pairs of clotted boots, the floor patterned with sloppy prints.

In the kitchen, wet and weary men crowded around the kitchen table, many standing, muddy to the knees, all but one in their stocking feet.

Here, in our very own kitchen, was a trooper from the

state barracks, the only one in the room with his boots still on. They reached to his knees and were mostly clean, so I knew he hadn't been in the woods all morning like the others. He creaked with leather: belt, boots, holster, chin strap. There was a row of long, sharp bullets tucked into loops in his belt. The handle of his gun was a smooth wood—almost pretty—his uniform stiff and sharp from hem to hat, except for some goofy pouches that stuck out from the sides of his trousers. *Aha*, I thought. *Jodhpurs.*

Constable Oleska was talking.

"... and every county bordering ours, but nobody's seen him. Of course, he's bound to be in the woods somewhere, more likely to be spotted by some hunter or a farmer. The word is out and it will spread. Someone will see him eventually and we'll get a chance to talk to him. But Officer Coleman is here to help us find Betty, not Toby."

I sidled around to stand by my grandmother, who was ladling out soup while my mother carried the hot bowls, one by one, to the men. I caught a glimpse of my brothers through the trooper's planted legs, huddled under the table, wide-eyed.

Officer Coleman had a deep voice, of course. It went well with his square chin and broad shoulders. He was a man straight out of a book.

"The constable is right," he said. "But we can't look

for Betty properly unless we know why she's missing. Shouldn't be looking for her at all, around here, if Toby's taken her."

And there it was again. That horrible suggestion. I wanted to yell, *He didn't! He's in the barn reading* Treasure Island! That would teach them a thing or two.

"Until we find him, and we will, we have to assume that Betty's just hurt and can't call for help. You could walk right past her in the leaves and mud and not see her at all."

"She was wearing a yellow poncho when she left her house yesterday," the constable said.

"Well, that's a blessing," the trooper said. "But you wouldn't see that if she were in an oil shack or down a well."

Inside, I went still.

I felt like someone had reached out and tapped me on the shoulder. Somewhere from my memory, a whisper.

"There are old pits in Wolf Hollow," my grandfather said. "Pretty much filled in, but maybe she stepped into a pocket and went down."

"We looked all around the hollow," Andy's father said.

I wondered where Andy was. Perhaps out searching, still.

"Keep looking," the trooper said. "If he took her, you won't find her. If he hurt her, though, you might find . . . something." He glanced at my mother over his shoulder. At me.

"You might find something," he repeated. "If she's still around here and just hurt, she might be unconscious. In one of those pits and can't answer your calls. Keep calling, though. Even if she can't answer, she might hear you and take heart."

"Wouldn't the dogs find her then?" This time it was Mr. Ansel asking the question. His accent, in this company, sounded stronger than ever.

The trooper shook his head. "Not your dogs, I'm afraid. And our hounds won't be here until later today if we're lucky. Maybe tomorrow. They're working a job in Waynesburg. But we'll be getting some help soon. People come from all over when there's a search on. In the meantime, we keep looking. And I want to talk to your son," he said to Andy's father.

Mr. Woodberry got a look on his face and said, "He didn't do nothin'."

"Well, nobody said he did, but I'm told he was close to the girl. With her before she disappeared. And he might know more than he thinks he knows."

The men were all eating their soup and rolls, settling down into the quiet business of food and rest, while the trooper talked some more. "Constable Oleska told me about the other troubles you've been having. The girl who lost an eye"—at which Mr. Ansel paused, his spoon halfway to his mouth. "Your son cut on a taut-wire." This addressed to my father. I saw James, under the table, reach up to finger the scab on his forehead.

"I found a coil of sharp wire in Toby's smokehouse, tucked under his bedding," Officer Coleman continued. "And there was blood on it."

My mother went still. She was standing next to me and I felt her change. Stiffen.

Again, I wanted to yell out, *Betty took it. Toby didn't hurt anybody.*

But I didn't. I needed time to think about all this. To listen to the whisper in the back of my mind.

I filled a mug with soup and ate it standing up, slowly as Toby had, listening to the men talk about where they'd been and what they'd seen. And for the first time I began to wonder in earnest where Betty had gone.

Until now, I had spent all my time fighting the suggestion that Toby had done her harm. I'd assumed that Betty was playing another of her stupid games, or that she had run off somewhere. But now I began to wonder where she really was and why no one had found her.

When the men had their fill, they went back out to continue the search, and this time I really did want to go with them. But I stayed behind to help with the dishes, a chore that always helped my thoughts settle, and hoped I'd hear that whisper again more clearly.

"Annabelle, if that plate gets any drier it's going to turn to dust," my grandmother said.

I looked down, surprised to see the same plate I'd been drying for quite some time.

"Sorry, Grandma. I wasn't paying attention."

"Not to that plate, anyway." She nodded at the rack of steaming dishes waiting their turn. "How about you get on with those." She still had a sink full of dishes meant for that rack.

I picked up a mug, dried it, picked up another, dried it. And so on, my hands with a mind of their own as I thought and thought and thought about the wire and the trooper and the rest of the mess.

When we were done with the dishes, I helped sweep up the dried mud in the kitchen from where the men had been, though the worse of it was in the mudroom. "Do what you can," my mother said. "But don't scrub anything. It will just get mucked up again at suppertime when they come back."

It was so unlike my mother to leave a mess that I realized, suddenly, how tired she was, too. And how worried.

"I'm sure they'll find Betty soon enough," I said.

She sighed. "I expect they will, one way or another."

Again, that suggestion of something worse to come.

Something everyone else seemed to expect.

I was glad that I didn't, though I was beginning to think that perhaps I should.

"Can I go out and look around some more?" I asked.

"Yes, I suppose so," she replied. "I was surprised when you didn't ask to go back out with the rest of them."

I tucked my broom into the closet. "I'm a little tired," I said, which was the truth. "But I would like to go on out for a while."

My mother nodded. "Same as before: Don't go far. Don't get in any trouble."

"I won't," I said, hoping I meant it. "I'll be back soon."

Toby was again hiding in the bales when I returned to the loft. I announced myself softly and then stopped short at the sight of him.

"I climbed down," he said nervously. "With everyone inside for lunch, I decided to clean up at the cistern, like you said."

He had trimmed his beard short, scrubbed himself clean, washed his hair so that it stuck up, featherlike, all around his head.

He looked . . . new.

In my father's clothes, he could have passed for anyone, really. An ordinary man, too thin, a little ragged, unremarkable but for the scars on his hand.

Having seen the transformation, I could not unsee it. Could not know if he was as changed as he seemed to be.

But it occurred to me—and I warmed, in the process, as if a small sun were rising—that no one else would know him as Toby, changed as he was.

"Golly," I said. "You look so different."

He looked down at himself. "I feel like a stranger."

I nodded. "You look like a stranger."

He sat on a bale and looked at me expectantly. "What?"

"What what?"

"You seem worried."

"Well, I am worried. I'm worried about all kinds of things. But I just got worried about something new."

"What?" he said again.

It was odd to feel like the grown-up, but that's how I felt as I stood up there in that loft and talked to this man who was four times my age.

"If I had a way to . . . let you . . . to help you clear things up, you know, about what Betty said . . . would you do it?"

Toby gnawed on that for a minute. "It would depend."

"On what?"

"On what you had in mind." He touched his short hair, as if he wore a new hat that didn't quite fit. "Everything's moving a little too fast for my liking as it is."

But I thought that fast was probably better than not at all, which was what he'd have done without me.

For the first time, I wondered if I had made things worse by trying to make them better.

"Well, you can wait here for as long as you want," I said. "And maybe they'll find Betty and realize you didn't do anything wrong."

Toby rubbed his bad hand and looked at me curiously. "Or?"

"Or you can do something about it."

He raised his eyebrows. "Such as?"

I spent a moment deciding where to begin.

"Last year," I said, "I walked up over the hill above our house, just at twilight, real quietly, hoping to see a mother and fawn I'd seen there before. I crept to the top of the hill and stood there for a long time, watching, but there weren't any deer anywhere. Until I batted at a fly and spooked a doe standing against the trees at the edge of the field. She was hiding in plain sight."

Toby peered at me. "That's a very nice story, Annabelle."

"I'm glad you liked it." I waited for the penny to drop.

He waited right along with me.

"You're the deer," I finally said.

"I'm the what?"

"You're the deer. You're the one who's hiding in plain sight." I realized he hadn't seen himself in a mirror, had no way of knowing how entirely he'd changed. "No one will know you're Toby, not like you look now."

He made a face. "Even if that's true, how is it going to help me fix anything?"

So I told him.

It took some convincing, but once Toby accepted the idea that no one would recognize him now, he began to see the possibilities.

We decided that he should stay in the barn until after dark, maybe morning, and then join the search. If anyone asked, he had come in from Hopewell to lend a hand. Had heard about our missing Betty and come to do what he could. And so on.

"This is starting to feel like a game," he said. "I don't like it."

"I don't either. This is all just a big dumb misunderstanding. But you really are the deer, Toby, and all those other men are the hunters. You can't hide forever, and I can't keep this secret for much longer. It's like a stone in my belly."

Toby nodded. "I know what that feels like."

He rubbed his bad hand over his face, seemed startled to find his beard so short.

I couldn't help but stare at his scars, so close and terrible.

He saw me staring, lowered his hand slowly, and held it out toward me.

"I don't mind," he said.

I'm sure he didn't mean for me to touch it, but after I had a long look at the ruined skin—as lumpy and veined as October cabbage—I took his hand in both of mine and turned it over, turned it back, my hands so little and soft in comparison.

When he started to pull away, I held fast.

When I looked up, I found that Toby was crying.

And then I was, too.

What Toby told me that afternoon I've never told another living soul.

Perhaps it had been such a long time since someone had touched him that those few moments of his hand in mine were enough to split him open.

What showed through the breach was so sad that I've never stopped wondering how he survived it.

He talked about the war.

"Not this war now," he said. "The other one. The one

that was supposed to be the last one."

I didn't understand a lot of what he said. Most of the time he wasn't even talking to me. Not really.

Just talking. Sometimes through his hands. Pacing. Telling a story.

About the "something bad" he'd done.

He talked about the sound a bullet makes as it pierces a skull.

The taste of dirt mixed with blood. The smell of it. How it feels to crouch in a muddy trench that shudders with bomb-blast and wonder if mustard gas is snaking across the ground above, closer each moment.

How a man bellows, cow-like, as he is cut to pieces. How another man whistles like a train.

He talked about what it was like to eat grass in a field, as if he were a horse, and to sleep in a tree, his gun belt a cinch, and to want to stay there forever, to starve there, his rib cage a home for nesting birds, his bones falling, one by one, as gravity released them, like dead branches.

He talked about the soldiers he'd shot. "So many," he said. "So many."

And he talked about a baby, just born, its belly still tethered to the womb, and the mother, too . . . beyond which he didn't say much that made any sense, if any of it had.

I tried to interrupt once or twice, to tell him that he

wasn't the terrible person he claimed to be, to promise him that God would understand, but it was as if I were one of the rock doves overhead, cooing in a language that made no sense to him.

So I held very still and waited, trying not to hear it all, hoping, even at just eleven, almost twelve, that I would never have sons of my own.

CHAPTER EIGHTEEN

When he wore himself out, Toby lay down in the hay and went to sleep at once. His lashes, wet against his cheeks, were more like a child's than I would have thought possible.

He slept without a sound. Without moving. And he didn't know when I covered him with his coat and left him there.

I climbed slowly out of the loft, nearly falling once, and made my way down the stairs, through the stable below, and out through the open gate.

It was odd, but everything had changed color. Just a little. Everything was sharper. Brighter.

As I passed the henhouse, one of the chickens clucked at me through the screen of its little window and I wanted to kiss the yellow thorn of its beak.

If only a dog had come blustering out of the woodshed to grant me passage, I would have lain down in the leaves and made him into a pillow. I would have stayed there and let his fur become my world for a while.

Instead, I saw a strange car parked in our lane. The trooper's car. And I buttoned my heart, took a deep breath, and gave myself a chore to do.

I was good at chores.

Entering my house helped. It was nothing else but what it was.

"Where's Officer Coleman?" I asked my mother from the mudroom.

She and my grandmother were making enough slaw for "a posse of Huns," one of many confusing things my grandfather liked to say.

"Oh, it's just his car that's still here, not him," my grandmother said. "It was easier for your grandpap to take him down to the Woodberrys' in our truck than to try to give him directions."

I stood in the kitchen doorway and watched them work. "So he's coming back here?"

"Soon, I would expect. They've been gone for quite a while."

"Annabelle, wash up and get started on these potatoes," my mother said. "All those men who've come to help look for Betty will need to be fed, and some of them are sure to tag along home with your father."

When I didn't move or answer, she turned to look me over. "Annabelle?" She wiped her hands on her apron and came to feel my cheeks. "Are you all right? You're so pale."

I nodded. "I feel fine."

She didn't look convinced. "Well, then wash your hands and come help."

I had meant to keep an eye on my brothers, making sure they didn't go anywhere near the barn, but they were so worn-out from searching that I found them lying on the sitting room floor, surrounded by Tinkertoys, listening to *The Adventures of Superman* on the radio.

I felt quite old as I watched them.

But then Officer Coleman came back with my grand-father, and in a trice I was a worried girl all over again.

At the sound of the trooper's big voice, my brothers crept into the kitchen and crawled under the table as before.

I tried very hard to listen properly to what Officer Coleman had learned from Andy, but it wasn't easy.

The sound of Toby's voice, the sight of him sleeping in the hay, muffled everything else, as if I were inside a Mason jar and not nearly enough holes in the lid for breathing.

Over hot coffee and pie, Officer Coleman told us the rest of the story, and I could see why Andy had held some back.

"He told me what he'd already told the constable. That he and Betty had meant to play hooky and meet up in the woods. But there was more to it than that. When I pushed him, he confessed that they'd made plans to go down to Cobb Hollow. If Toby was in his smokehouse, they'd go someplace else. If not, they meant to have a look around."

"Oh, for pity's sake," my mother said. "Why in the world would they do that?"

"You might well wonder," the trooper said, shaking his head. "It took some digging, but Andy's father is a hard man who, well, *encouraged* his son to cooperate. So Andy told us that they had decided to make some trouble for Toby that day. Maybe even set fire to his place, drive him away."

"I told you she was like that," I said, but my mother shushed me.

"You can be quiet, Annabelle, or you can get started on those potatoes."

The trooper gave me a small smile. "I'm not sure what to make of all this. Constable Oleska filled me in as much as he could, but it feels like a circus, the other business that's been going on. All I really want to do is find the girl."

"Andy wasn't any more help than that?" my grandmother asked.

"Not much." Officer Coleman pushed his plate away and finished the last of his coffee. "It was raining so hard the day she disappeared that Andy never imagined she'd be anywhere but school or home. When I asked him, he said he didn't think she would have gone down to the smokehouse alone. But she was the one who'd had the idea to devil Toby and drive him away. She was dead set on it. And now she's gone. And Toby's gone. And I think it's time I looked harder for him, instead of her."

He stood up and put his hat back on. "I thank you for your hospitality, ma'am," he said to my mother. "And for your help," he said to my grandfather; "and yours," he said to me; "... and yours," he said, bowing to peer under the table at Henry and James. "I'm sure the constable can manage the search from here on in."

And he left. Just like that.

I felt relieved, of course, that he'd be looking for Toby somewhere else. And I trusted that Constable Oleska would sort out what to do next. But he didn't know all the things that I knew.

He didn't know that Betty had thrown that rock,

regardless of the story that the picture or Betty herself had told.

He didn't know that Toby hadn't taken her.

He didn't know that the bloody wire they'd found in the smokehouse didn't mean a thing. That Betty had put it there. I was sure of it.

Which meant that she had indeed gone down to the smokehouse on the day she disappeared. While Toby was fishing under the creek bridge. While the rain came down in curtains.

And that's when the whisper in my head got louder. And I thought I knew where Betty was.

"Potatoes, Annabelle," my mother said. "Your father could be back anytime, and company with him."

"Yes, ma'am," I said.

The sink was full of huge potatoes, far easier to peel than small ones, and I let my hands do the work as the whisper gathered strength.

I tried to poke holes in my theory, but it had a pretty tight skin. Every question I asked myself had an answer. Every doubt a promise: She had to be there. It made sense that she was.

I was tempted to tell someone right then and there. To fix what was wrong without any more delay or confusion.

Finding Betty wouldn't clear Toby, though.

She had lied before and she would lie again, saying things that nobody could prove untrue. How was Toby supposed to prove that he hadn't hurt Ruth or James or Betty herself? How was he supposed to explain why he'd been hiding out if he wasn't guilty of those things?

I should have left him in his smokehouse. I should have left everything alone. What if he was forced to leave, now, with winter coming on?

"Annabelle, when you finish with those potatoes, go fetch me a jar of peaches from the cellar."

"Yes, ma'am," I said.

Chores first. Then whatever news my father brought home with him. And then, perhaps, I would tell them.

When my father came through the door an hour later, he looked more than weary. "I don't know where that girl is," he said as he took off his boots. "But if she's anywhere around here, she's out of sight and earshot."

A moment later, four other men, two of them strangers to me, came filing in, equally worn-out. Two of them were Mr. Earl and Mr. Jim. I couldn't remember their last names, but I knew that Mr. Earl was a mechanic and Mr. Jim was a grocer. My father introduced the newcomers: a Theodore Lester from Aliquippa, and Carl Anderson all the way from New Castle.

We said our hellos and how-do-you-dos, and my mother poured coffee for everyone while I set places at the table.

"I don't know what more we can do, Sarah," my father said. "The Glengarrys are beside themselves. Betty's mother has come, and she's been, well, hard on them for letting this happen."

"But that's not at all fair," my grandmother said.

"Not much about this that's fair," he said.

The afternoon was blending into evening, Aunt Lily would be home soon, and if I needed another reason to head for the barn, I soon had it.

"The constable ought to be back by now with a couple of bloodhounds from Waynesburg," my father said as he sat down with the others to a supper of beef with roasted potatoes and carrots. Stick-to-your-ribs food. Something Toby sorely needed, and I vowed to get some out to the barn as soon as I could. "They found a little boy stuck in a game trap in an old coal mine shaft, been missing for two days. But now they're ours and I believe we'll get somewhere in short order."

I should have been glad. If Betty was where I thought she was, they would find her, which was important. Of course that had to be the most important thing. And if it was—and I knew it was, it had to be—then the worst part of this would be over soon, one way or another.

Or I could just stand up right now and say, "I think I know where Betty is."

I almost did. The words leaned out of my mouth and nearly made the jump, but talking to Toby first seemed a better idea.

At the very least, he would have something to say about what happened next.

There was still some light left in the sky.

Soon, the men would go back out with those dogs.

I slipped into the mudroom and put on my coat and boots, rummaged through the closet until I found an old wool plaid hunting coat my grandfather hadn't worn for some time, stuffed some gloves in its pocket, and slipped out the mudroom door. Behind me, I heard my mother calling my name, but I kept going, out and down around the house and into the woods, as fast as I could.

The horses and cows were all waiting for me when I came through the back of the barn and into the middle aisle.

"You good girls," I said to the milk cows, opening the gate to their big stall and pulling some fresh hay out of their net and into the manger. The horses waited patiently, Dinah with her big head resting on Bill's back. "Sleepy girl. You come on in and settle down." I gave her a scoop of oats, tucked Bill into his stall and fed him, too.

Made sure their water buckets were full. And left them to their own devices.

Toby was awake when I reached the loft. He was sitting in the shadows, his head in his hands.

I waited for him to look up at me. When he did, I was shocked at his sad white face.

"I don't know why I did that," he said. "I never meant to do that, Annabelle."

"Do what?" I said.

"You ought not to have heard those things I said."

I put my hands on my hips. "Because I'm a girl?"

He shrugged and said, "Yes, Annabelle. Because you're a girl. But I would feel the same if it had been Henry or, even worse, James. If I could unlearn what I know, I would. In the blink of an eye. But I can't. And piling it on your head won't change that."

"My mother says I have a hard head." I tried to smile. "Besides, I'd rather know too much than too little."

I didn't tell him that I'd put his awful stories in boxes and stacked them on a shelf at the back of my mind. I could hear a quieter version of them still, from their dark place, through all the other business that occupied my brain, but I wouldn't unlid those boxes until I was ready to hear Toby's stories again as they wanted to be heard. And I didn't think that would happen for a long time.

I handed Toby my grandpap's old coat. "Put this on," I said.

He took it. "Why?"

"Because I have an idea, and if you don't think it's too stupid, we're going to go right now and try it out."

I told Toby what Andy had said, about Betty's plan to make mischief at the smokehouse, maybe burn it down so he'd have no home at all.

Toby rubbed his bad hand with his good one. "Why does she hate me so much?" he said.

"I don't think she does, Toby, but you're the perfect person to blame. Betty throws a rock. She blames it on you. Betty sets a taut-wire. Blames it on you." I told him how the trooper had found the bloody wire in the smokehouse.

"Sounds like hate to me," he said.

"I know," I said. "I felt that way, too, but I don't think it's hate. I think it's more like she just does stuff."

And then I told him where I thought Betty might be and what we should do about it.

"I maybe haven't been all that careful so far," I said, "jumping around like a blind frog. But I think you have to be the one to save her."

He asked me some questions. Considered the idea in silence. Asked me some more questions.

"It's not stupid," he said. "But finding her isn't going to solve everything. She'll just tell more lies."

"You're right," I said. "They might blame you on her say-so. They might arrest you. Or you might have to just keep on walking, straight out of here, and start over somewhere else. But even if saving her doesn't clear your name, it will still be a good thing, Toby."

He nodded.

In my grandfather's plaid hunting coat, Toby looked even less like himself. His black oilcloth coat lay draped over a bale of hay like a giant bat. His old hat, full of the hair I'd cut, looked fit for nothing but the fire. Without them, he would be known only by what he did that night.

But then he reached for his guns.

"What are you doing?" I said. "You can't go around with those on your back. That'll ruin everything. Even one gun across your back will seem pretty strange, but three and you're Toby again."

He clenched his hands together so tightly that his scars went as white as milk.

"Are you afraid of bears?" I asked. That, at least, I could understand.

"No," he said.

"Then why carry those guns everywhere? Don't they get awfully heavy?"

He unclenched his hands and rubbed them together as if they were cold. "They do," he said.

"Then why do you carry them?"

I waited.

"Because I do," he said.

"You sound like James."

He didn't seem to mind the comparison. And it didn't prompt a better explanation.

I knew there was one in Toby's awful stories, waiting in their boxes. Someday, I'd listen harder.

For now, I headed down the ladder.

When Toby followed, without even pausing at the top, he had no guns across his back.

CHAPTER NINETEEN

The men were just leaving the house when I returned.

"Annabelle, where have you been?" my father said. "Your mother needs you inside."

"I went to let the animals into their stalls."

My grandfather started up our truck while the others piled into the flatbed, a company of mutts with them.

"Well, good," my father said, turning away. "Now go on inside and help your mother."

"Wait," I said, following him across the lane. "Daddy, wait a minute."

"Annabelle, we've got to get going," he said as he opened the cab door. "The light's almost gone and the bloodhounds are out at the church, ready to go."

"Daddy, I think I know where Betty is."

Which stopped him cold. He closed the truck door.

"You know where she is?" He sounded, looked askance, and I couldn't blame him. "Just like that?"

"I was filling the horse buckets, at the cistern, and I remembered something." The lie seemed so small compared to everything else. "Andy told the trooper that Betty meant to go down to Toby's place and cause some trouble. So I figured maybe she *did* go down there when Andy didn't show up at the Turtle Stone."

My father shook his head impatiently.

"Annabelle, Constable Oleska went down there looking for Toby. Betty wasn't there. And the trooper went down there himself and had a good look around. She wasn't there. She isn't there, Annabelle."

"But they were looking for Toby. They weren't really looking for Betty because that was before they knew she might have gone down there. To cause trouble for him."

My father opened the door to the truck again. "I don't understand what you're getting at, Annabelle. That shack is one room. There's no cellar. There's no attic. There's no closet. And there was no sign that she'd been there."

"Except that wire."

"Annabelle—"

"She didn't see anything from the belfry, Daddy. Toby didn't do anything wrong."

191

My father climbed into the truck. "Annabelle, I have to go."

"Daddy, she's in the well," I said.

He shook his head. "Toby doesn't have a well." He began to shut the door.

"Yes, he does," I said, grabbing his arm. "There's one back in the woods at the old Cobb place."

"Annabelle," my mother called from the doorway.

"It's just a hole in the ground," I said. "You could walk right past it."

My father went still. "I'm sure someone has searched every square inch around there."

"Betty said she was afraid of Toby," I reminded him. "Nobody thought she'd be anywhere near the smokehouse. Andy was the only one who knew she wanted to go down there that day."

I couldn't tell him about the odd sounds I'd heard in the dark. Like a frightened animal.

"Annabelle!" my mother called again.

"I'm going with Daddy," I called back.

"Go on inside," he said. "We'll have a look in the well."

"Please, let me come along," I begged. "I won't get in the way. I promise."

He considered me for a moment and then waved an okay to my mother.

I climbed into the truck and sat between him and my grandfather, who was, thankfully, a slow and careful driver.

By the time we got to the church, Toby would be getting close to Cobb Hollow.

By the time my father told the handlers to keep the dogs leashed for the time being, Toby would be headed down the slope toward his smokehouse.

By the time my father had told the constable to follow us down to Cobb Hollow, Toby would be waiting for us in the woods with night coming quickly on.

And by the time we found the well, Toby would be ready to join us, just one more stranger come to help, blending in like a chameleon.

As we drove down the lane into Cobb Hollow, I recalled once more the sound I'd heard. A porcupine, I'd thought.

I pictured Betty trapped deep in that cold well for two days, the rain pouring in on top of her, and I wasn't sure she'd need more punishing for all she'd done. But I knew that Ruth might disagree.

My grandfather pulled the truck down the Cobb lane and parked by Toby's smokehouse. Another truck pulled in behind him, the constable at the wheel, five more men with him.

We all piled out and gathered in the clearing.

"There's a well in those woods," my father called out, "back down the lane some and off to the left. Watch where you step."

He grabbed my sleeve. "You stay right with me, Annabelle, you understand?"

I did. I *wanted* to be with him. If Betty wasn't in that well, if I was wrong about that, I didn't know what I'd do. And somewhere nearby, Toby was waiting to see what happened. I had to be close. I had to be the one to help him, if it came to that. And I wanted my father with me.

The men fanned out and started through the trees. It was dark enough so one by one the flashlights came on, bobbing and shifting, guiding us forward.

The burned-out foundation of the Cobb house was easy to find, but it took longer to locate the well itself, which was nothing more than a dark spot on the ground, the flat stones around it long buried in moss and rot.

By rights, the hole, too, should have been covered over with leaves by now. And I knew, without looking in, that it had been. That Betty had stepped on it, unawares, and that her falling body had cleared it for us to find.

I stepped back as the men converged around it. How horrible. How horrible. How horrible that she could be in there. That anyone could be in there.

I hadn't thought about it before. Not really. Or I would

have screamed it out and run to find her.

The constable stepped to the edge and shined his flashlight straight down into the hole.

"I can't see anything," he said. "John."

My father joined him, two others as well, and they made a circle around the well and pointed their lights together down the hole.

"My Lord, she's down there," the constable said. "Betty!"

And then it was all confusion as the men scrambled to the trucks for lanterns and rope and shovels.

I stood clear, my back against a tree.

I watched as Toby came out of the darkness and into the fray without a word. Nobody noticed anything but here were two more hands to help pull her out of that well.

He was wearing my grandfather's old gloves.

He looked like a farmer. Like my father. Like Henry or James would look someday.

In the end, it took a while to get Betty free.

It was a dug well, once roomy enough for a man with a shovel, but then narrowed by the laid stone he'd used to line it. Betty was only about twenty feet down, the front of her poncho caught on a rusty old pipe. Cradled in it as if from a stork's beak, she had been saved from falling all the way to the bottom, but her legs hung down out of sight, and we all wondered if they hung in November water.

The men were worried about dislodging her, sending her deeper into the well, hurting her worse or even drowning her. But they knew they had to get her out of there as quickly as possible.

They called to her again and again, but she did not respond when they dangled a rope down to her, and there was no way she could tie it around herself in any event.

On the other side of the well from where I stood with my father, Toby and the others watched. I met his eyes across that dreadful breach. In the lantern light, he looked younger but even more serious than he ever had in his beard and black coat and hat.

"Someone needs to go down there and get her out," my father said.

"Yes, but we really ought to use a tripod and a winch," the constable said. "We do this wrong and the man we lower could end up falling in with her."

"You want to wait while someone goes after a winch?" my father said.

"No," the constable said. "No, I don't. And I'm sure Betty doesn't want to be down there for one minute longer than she has to be."

I remembered the hours I'd spent picking milkweed

pods, cutting Toby's hair. I remembered chatting with the horses as I gave them their oats. I remembered being glad that my grandfather was a slow and careful driver. And I felt sick.

An oak standing near the well reached out above it with a sturdy limb. We all stepped back as my father tied a heavy knot in one end of the rope and tossed it over the branch to the constable, who pulled it down and looped it into a quick harness.

"I'll go," my father said, unbuttoning his coat.

But Toby, standing next to the constable, took the rope out of his hands. "Let me," he said. "I'm skinny, but I'm strong." He kept his gloves on but shed my grandfather's coat.

"I don't know you," the constable said, but he sounded nothing more than curious.

"I'm not from around here," Toby said. "But I came to help, and I'd be obliged if you'd let me."

I began to breathe again, though I realized that my hands were in fists as my father and the constable fit the harness around Toby, leaving a long tail that he could use to secure Betty.

"You sure about this?" the constable asked him. "She's putting weight on the wall where she's caught. No telling whether the whole thing might not collapse and take you with it."

The other men had made a ring around the well. I could see between them. Toby, adjusting the harness. Looking at the constable, nodding his response.

"Take my flashlight," the constable said. "We won't be able to shine any light down past you, but I don't know how you're going to get her tied and hold the flashlight without another hand or two."

"I'll manage," Toby said. He reached into his pocket and handed my father his jackknife. "Would you hold this for me? I'll be going in upside down, so . . ."

"You have a wallet? Keys?"

Toby paused for a moment. Then, "In my coat."

As Toby knelt at the edge of the well, my father said, "I didn't catch your name."

Toby looked back over his shoulder. "Jordan," he said. And it felt like the truth.

By now, someone had fetched the Glengarrys, and they arrived in a state of panic, Betty's mother a surprise in city clothes and pin curls. She cried a little as all the men lined up along the rope and slowly lowered Toby headfirst into the well. The oak limb bowed some, but it held, and the rope was thick enough to stand some fraying as his weight dragged it hard against the bark.

They lowered him, hand over hand, until Toby called

out a muffled *whoa!*, which the constable echoed, his hand in the air. "He's got to her," he called. "Stop and hold it steady."

We waited, the rope shivering. I pictured him tucking the flashlight under his chin, looping the rope around her.

I heard him yell something else.

"He can't get the rope under her arms," the constable said. "She's swaddled in that poncho. But if he moves it out of the way it might come off that pipe."

My father had his flashlight trained down the well, a lantern high in his other hand. "He's going to have to grab her and pull her out himself."

"Can you get your arms around her?" the constable called into the well.

A long pause. The rope shivered some more. The men holding it leaned back against the pull.

That's when we knew how badly Betty was hurt.

From deep in the well, she screamed.

It wasn't like anything I'd ever heard before.

Betty's grandmother turned in tight circles, her head bowed, hands in fists against her mouth.

I said my prayers, found it impossible that I'd waited for even one minute before telling my father what I'd gleaned from that soft whisper: *That was no porcupine you heard.*

And I understood, in the tiniest, palest measure, why Toby carried those guns wherever he went.

Above the well, the rope tightened and thrummed. "Hold steady!" the constable called again. He dropped to his knees and leaned into the well. Toby was yelling something, but I couldn't make out a word of it.

"She's stuck," the constable said, looking up at my father. "When her poncho caught on that pipe, she must have slammed back against the other side of the well. There's a second pipe coming out just there behind her and she's stuck on it."

My father leaned in closer above the hole. "What do you mean, stuck on it?"

"It impaled her," the constable said. "It's through her shoulder."

I closed my eyes. There, in that moment, I thought I would never care about any small nonsense ever again.

And Betty screamed. And screamed.

"He's pulling her off the pipe," the constable said and, to the men on the rope line, yelled, "Get ready! He's going to be taking her weight."

But they still flinched, as one, when the rope tried to cope with its new burden, the branch bowed overhead, and the constable yelled, "Now heave but slowly!" standing again and signaling with his arm to heave, heave, heave until up came Toby's feet, his legs, all of him slowly up into the lantern light, and in his arms, tight against his chest and neck, a bundle of wet rags and matted hair, blue lips, blood streaming off the poncho, her legs drenched and limp, her face so white that I did not see how she could be alive.

They laid Betty gently on a nest of coats in the flatbed of the constable's truck. She was conscious, but barely. When her teeth began to chatter, I was startled to find myself thinking again of a wild animal. Groundhogs chattered their teeth like that when the dogs had them cornered.

I pinched myself hard on the soft skin just under my chin.

As Betty's grandfather covered her with his coat, I noticed that she was wearing her poncho inside out, the dark lining on the outside, the yellow hidden. And I pictured her creeping through Cobb Hollow, into Toby's smokehouse, tucking the coil of wire under his bedding.

I pinched myself again and turned away.

It was impossible to know just how badly Betty was hurt, but we all knew that she needed to get to a hospital quickly. Where she had been impaled, her flesh was already green and swollen. And while she could wiggle her fingers, she couldn't seem to move her legs.

"She's been cold and still for a long time," my father said. "It may be that she just needs warming."

Betty's mother climbed into the front of the constable's truck while her grandparents and two men from the rope line took up spots in the back to hold Betty still.

When another of the men offered to take Mrs. Glengarry's place, she waved him off. "Thank you," she said. "But no."

If it was possible to hurry slowly, that's just what the constable did as he started the truck and ferried Betty off and away.

And that left the rest of us to stand in a pool of lantern light and stare at one another, catching our breath and trying to slow ourselves down.

"I'm Jed Hopkins," one of the men said, holding his hand out until Toby took it. "That was really something, what you did."

"It was," said another man, offering his hand and his name, and then each of them, in turn, thanked Toby for what he'd done.

"We've all been spared a nightmare or two, Jordan, though I'm afraid you'll have them for us," my father said. "I'm John McBride. And this is my daughter, Annabelle."

"Pleased to meet you both," Toby said. He was careful not to look straight at me.

We spent a few minutes coiling rope and covering the well with branches until it could be properly capped.

Then, "I guess we can go on home," my father said.

"I guess," I replied, looking around for Toby. I saw him standing near his smokehouse, his back to me.

"You all," my father said to the others, "I'll give you a ride back to your trucks and you can go on home from there."

"What about him?" I whispered, nodding toward Toby.

"Jordan?" my father said. "A stranger who asked us to lower him into a well to save a girl he'd never met? He's coming home with us."

CHAPTER TWENTY

Toby rode in the back of the truck with the dogs and four other men, some from our hills, some from farther afield. At the church, they climbed out and headed for their own trucks. My father yelled our thanks out the window, and they waved and smiled and went back to their lives with a story that their children's children would tell well into another century.

From there to the farm, Toby rode alone in the back, at his insistence. When I turned and looked through the cab window, I could see him huddled with the dogs just on the other side of the glass, once again buttoned into my grandfather's old coat, still gloved, but surely bone-chilled by the dark wind and what he'd seen and done inside that well.

When we arrived at the farmhouse, Toby hesitated,

but my father and I both stood in the lane and waited for him to join us while the dogs took off for the woodshed. "Come on in and have something to eat," my father said. "Can't send you home hungry after what you just did."

My brothers hurried to the door to greet us. They were freshly bathed, rosy and warm, their hair wet-dark around their faces, and I wanted to hug them to me and cry. But I didn't. If I had tried, they surely would have wrestled me to the floor and pronounced me a girl.

But I loved them in a way that didn't need proving.

My father took Toby's coat and hung it in the closet where it had, just that morning, belonged.

"Your gloves?" my father said, but Toby tucked his hands under his arms and said softly, looking at the floor, "Still pretty cold." Which made sense. "I'll keep them on a bit longer, if you don't mind."

"Hard to eat with your gloves on, but I do know something about cold hands," my father said, smiling.

Everyone had gathered in the kitchen at the sound of us coming in. To all of them, my father said, "This is Jordan. Jordan, these are my parents, Daniel and Mary. My sister, Lily."

Aunt Lily stepped forward and held out her hand, giving him a rare smile. "How do you do?" she said in a soft voice I didn't know she had.

Toby hesitated for a moment and then took off his glove and shook her hand. "Pleased to meet you," he said, and put his glove back on.

"James and Henry," my father said, nodding at the boys. "Jordan, what should they call you, Mr.—"

"Jordan is fine," he said.

And the boys said, in tandem, "Did you find Betty?" and "Is she dead?"

"Oh, hush," Aunt Lily said.

"And my wife, Sarah."

Toby stood with my father and me, in the wide doorway between the mudroom and the kitchen, and actually bowed, as if he were a musketeer.

"Hello," he said.

My mother had gone still at the sound of Toby's voice. Now, at this odd behavior, she wiped her hands on her apron and stepped forward. "Your name is Jordan?"

"It is," he said.

She looked into his face, and I thought that she might know.

"Come. Sit," she said, leading him to the table.

While my mother warmed up food left over from supper, my father told the story.

I helped a little.

Toby said nothing at all. Even when my father explained how they'd lowered him into the well, and Aunt Lily said, "That was very brave of you, Jordan," again in that soft, almost-musical voice . . . and the boys launched a barrage of questions about what it was like and were there snakes and centipedes and did the well go all the way to China.

They stopped when my father got to the part about Betty.

No one said a word as he described the situation, but when he had finished, my grandmother excused herself quietly and went off to bed.

"I'll say my good nights now, too," my grandfather said. He turned to Toby. "I hope you'll take a peck of apples when you go."

"Thank you," Toby said. "I will."

My mother poured more coffee for him and my father.

"Can I have some, too?" I asked, but she ignored me.

"Is Betty going to be all right?" she said.

"I can't say. But the constable took her to the hospital, so I'm sure he'll have some news before long."

"And what about that Toby," Aunt Lily asked. "Have they found *him* yet?"

I glanced at Toby and away. Caught my mother's eyes on me.

"Not that I know of," my father said. "But it seems

clear that Betty went down to Toby's place to make mischief and simply fell into the old Cobb well."

"Then where is he?" Aunt Lily said.

"That's enough about that," my mother said, setting places for my father and Toby and me. "Let's just be glad that Betty's found." She put a platter of beef and potatoes and carrots on the table. "Please," she said to Toby. "Help yourself."

When, as before, he hesitated, she took his plate and served him. "Now eat up while it's hot," she said.

I held my breath, but Toby simply pulled the glove off his right hand and began to eat. I hoped no one else noticed when he returned his left hand, still gloved, to his lap, cutting his meat one-handed with the edge of his fork.

Aunt Lily got up from the table and said, "Well, if you'll all excuse me, I have work early in the morning." She turned to Toby and smiled again. "It was so very nice to meet you, Jordan. I hope we'll see you again sometime."

Toby rose partway out of his seat. "Likewise."

"Oh," she said, caught by an afterthought. "John, you didn't tell us how you came to discover that Betty was in the well. Was it the bloodhounds?"

My father pointed a fork at me and said, "It was *that* bloodhound. Our very own Sherlock Holmes figured it out."

Aunt Lily was the only person I knew who could raise

just one eyebrow, which had the effect of making her look both skeptical and wise. "And how did you do that, Annabelle?"

I shrugged. "I just spent the day thinking about what Andy said, that's all." I looked straight at her. "And I knew Toby didn't do anything wrong, which made it easier to sort out what really happened."

Aunt Lily pursed her lips and lifted her chin. "Your faith in that man is a mystery to me, Annabelle. He's hurt two little girls—Ruth and Betty both—and maybe others."

"Time for bed, boys," my father said, which triggered the usual protests and the equally customary reaction from Aunt Lily.

"Right now," she barked, shepherding them from the table. They fled as she advanced. Like the rest of us, they knew that Aunt Lily wasn't afraid to bite.

Now it was just us four. My mother poured herself a cup of coffee and sat at the table, watching us eat.

"Where are you from, Jordan?" she asked Toby.

He glanced at me, then turned to her. "Maryland, originally. But I live in Hopewell now."

"And you heard that Betty was missing?"

Toby nodded slowly. "Word about something like that travels fast."

"And what do you do for a living?" my mother asked. I heard a growing thread of challenge in her voice, though I may have been sewing it there myself. Toby was so clearly Toby to me that I didn't see how the others could miss it.

"I'm a carpenter," he said.

Like "Jordan" and "Maryland," this had a ring of truth to it.

"Your wife must be worried about you by now," my mother said, her elbows on the table, both hands around her coffee cup. She looked at him steadily through a drift of rising steam.

I knew she could not have seen his left hand—and therefore could not have seen a wedding band.

"You can call her if you like," my father said.

"I'm not married," Toby said softly. He looked so uncomfortable when he said it that my mother stopped her questioning, but she kept her eyes on him for another long moment.

"Save some room for dessert," she said. "I made a hickory nut pie."

When the telephone rang a moment later, we weren't as surprised as we might have been.

"That's the constable," my father said. "He promised to call when there was news."

He went into the sitting room, and we could hear him talking, though not what he said.

My mother sighed. "I hope she's all right. Nobody deserves what she got."

"Not for what she did," Toby said.

I looked up sharply.

My mother tipped her head and regarded him curiously. "And just what did she do?"

What she was asking, without asking, was clear: *How does a stranger from Hopewell know what Betty did or didn't do?*

My father saved Toby from answering. "Well," he said, sitting heavily at the table again and running a hand through his hair, "they've only just begun to discover all the things that might be wrong with Betty, but they know a few already. Her shoulder is all torn up from that pipe, and they're going to start treating her for tetanus and a pretty bad infection. Still warming her up. Giving her blood."

My mother took a long breath. "No broken bones?"

My father shook his head. "Amazingly, no, but there's some gangrene in her right foot. Her leg was wedged up tight under that poncho. When she tried to move it, the poncho started to rip, so she stopped. But they think it will be okay. She may lose a toe. Too soon to tell."

I felt sick. "So she's talking about it?"

"Yes. A little." He looked away. "She's talking about Toby. She's saying he pushed her down that well."

"But—"

"Just hold on, Annabelle. I'm just saying what *she* said. No point arguing with me about it."

"But she's lying!"

"Let your father speak, Annabelle."

"She's saying that Toby caught her snooping around Cobb Hollow yesterday morning before the rain got too bad. Grabbed her. Put her in the smokehouse."

Toby had bowed his head, both hands in his lap. I stared at him, afraid of what he might be thinking. I could see places where I'd been careless with his hair. A small cowlick on his crown. An unevenness.

"She said he was angry that she had ratted on him. About throwing the rock that hit Ruth. About the taut-wire. And that after he packed up his things, he dragged her into the woods and pushed her down the well without a word. Just like that."

"And took off," my mother said.

"And took off."

Here was everything I'd feared. How was Toby supposed to prove something he *hadn't done*?

By now, Mrs. Gribble would be spreading the news down every telephone line on her switchboard, tapped like

212

an octopus into houses all over these hills.

Within the hour, Toby would be a murderous monster and Betty a poor dear thing.

In the silence that followed, I watched my mother trace the grain of the tabletop with her finger as if she were reading a map.

"Well, I certainly do want to thank you for your help tonight, Jordan," my father said. "When you're ready, I can take you back to wherever you've left your car. We have some apples in the—"

"John," my mother interrupted.

He stopped short. "What?"

My mother looked from Jordan to my father.

"He doesn't have a car," she said.

She gave my father a little smile, though it was sad, perhaps because the relief we'd all felt at Betty's rescue was to be so quickly replaced by more trouble.

"How do you know that?"

She turned to Toby. "Let me see your hands," she said.

I let out the breath I'd been holding in for two days.

"Sarah?" My father looked so confused that I wasn't sure whether to laugh or cry.

Toby sat up straight. He lifted his hands from his lap. With his bare right hand, he pulled off his other glove. The scars on his left hand were as irrefutable as a fingerprint.

"Jordan?" my father said, leaning closer.

"That's not his name," my mother said.

"It is, though," Toby said. "My name is Tobias Jordan. I am a carpenter from Maryland. And I did not push Betty down that well."

CHAPTER TWENTY-ONE

I could have escaped then.

Toby was the only one who knew that I'd been hiding him. The clothes he was wearing were more or less exactly the same as all the men wore, and it would be a while before my father missed them. I would have more than enough time to deal with the Mason jars, the camera, the scissors, and other things still in the hayloft. And I knew that Toby would never give me up. He'd say he'd taken the clothes from a laundry line, cut his own hair and beard, crept into our barn of his own accord.

"Toby didn't run off," I said. "I made him come with me. And he didn't hide. I hid him. In our barn. And I cut his hair and gave him some of your clothes to wear, Daddy. And he wouldn't have done any of that if I hadn't made him."

Though my mother had found Toby out, she looked shocked at these admissions. My father, too, was speechless.

"She was trying to help me," Toby said. "You can't be angry with her."

"I most certainly can," my mother said. "But I'm not. Not yet. I'll get to that soon."

"I can't believe you're Toby," my father said, staring at him wide-eyed. "You look so . . . different."

"But he's really not, Daddy."

"Well, yes he is," my father said.

"Yes, I am," Toby said. "Though that has nothing to do with it. I didn't do what Betty says I did. None of it." He stood up and pushed back his chair. "But I had better go before I make things worse for you all."

As I began to object, my mother said, "Sit down. I for one need a minute or two to sort things out. Good grief. The trooper was right. It is like a circus around here." She tucked a strand of stray hair behind her ear. "Besides," she said. "I made a pie and we are going to eat it if it's the last thing we do."

She got up from the table and began to dish out the pie, this time with whipped cream on top, as if it were Christmas.

"Wait for the coffee," she said as she put the pie on

the table. Which we did. My mother was using her don't-argue-with-me voice. The same one I'd used on Toby to get us here, to this table.

She gave me a glass of milk, more coffee for the men. "Well, go on," she said. "That pie's not going to eat itself."

Toby ate his piece slowly. Made it last long after we had finished ours. We sat and watched him as if he were a giraffe or a Martian. Even I had trouble believing that Toby was sitting at our kitchen table, eating pie, after years of avoiding any but brief contact with us, barely speaking, never allowing a soul to see him without his dark trappings.

"Help me understand this," my father finally said when Toby had finished his last bite, eyes closed. "I don't see how Annabelle . . . *spirited* you away from under our very noses. The constable has been looking for you since yesterday."

Toby shrugged. "I was fishing under the creek bridge all through the rainy part of the day, and then I was at the Turner place for jerky, and then back home after dark—"

"*After* Constable Oleska had been to the smokehouse and gone—" I said.

"And I hung up my wet things and went to sleep. Didn't know about Betty being missing until Annabelle knocked on my door before sunrise and told me what was going on and why I should go with her." He almost smiled at my mother, but she did not yet look inclined to smile back. "She sounded like you did just now."

My father couldn't help but grin at that, though briefly. "I know that voice," he said, mostly to himself.

"You're going to know it even better if you're not careful," my mother said.

"So you've been in the barn since . . ."

"Very early this morning." Toby ran his good hand through his beard and down his throat. "Seems like a long time ago."

"You went down there in the dark by yourself to get him?" my father said to me.

I nodded, split between pride and guilt. "I couldn't sleep and I knew how bad it looked. Don't you think that the trooper would have taken Toby away if I hadn't?"

Which was an argument that no one bothered to refute. We all knew what people thought of Toby, Aunt Lily and the Glengarrys among them.

"And then?" my mother said.

"I hid him in the hayloft. Took him some food and water. A book. Some clothes. Soap. I borrowed your scissors to give him a trim."

"And Jordan was born," she said thoughtfully.

"We didn't plan it out like that," I said. "And we didn't plan to go down to Cobb Hollow again, either. But I remembered a sound I'd heard in the dark last night, by the smokehouse. At the time, I thought it was a porcupine. But later, when the trooper told us what Andy said, about Betty wanting to go down there, I thought . . . what if she did? What if that's where she was? And I thought some more about the porcupine sound. And I remembered the well."

We sat silently for a little bit, looking at one another.

My father crossed his arms over his chest. "Who decided that Toby should join the rescue effort?"

"I did," I said, again not sure if it was all right to feel clever about it. "I was pretty sure he would blend in with the other strangers and be able to watch how things played out. Keep on going if he had to. Stay if he could."

I looked at each of them in turn. "But he can't, can he?" I said.

My father sighed. "I don't know, Annabelle. This is a mess, start to finish. And there's something else." From the way he frowned at Toby, I knew this couldn't be good. "The constable told me when he called just now that the hunt has intensified."

Toby frowned right back at him, clearly baffled. "But we found Betty."

"Not the search for Betty," my father said. "The hunt for you."

For the next hour we talked about what to do and how to keep what was now *our* secret until we had found a way to make things right.

But soon the day caught up with us, me especially. I'd been going since the wee hours of the morning, and I felt like a bag of rocks. Toby, more accustomed to little sleep and plenty of motion, was nonetheless a wreck himself.

"I still think I should leave right now," he said. "I can be twenty miles from here by morning."

"Which is exactly where they're looking," my father said. "And I don't see you walking twenty miles in the shape you're in."

My mother had fetched two blankets and a pillow, which she now handed to Toby.

"It won't be very warm out in the hayloft," she said, "but I think it's the only safe place for you right now."

"The loft will be fine," he said. "It smells good up there. And I like the doves."

"And here's some bread and cheese for the morning. Annabelle can bring you coffee before she goes to school."

The idea of school amazed me. But I knew I had to go. Nothing could call attention to us or our farm. Everything had to be as it always was.

"Good night," I said, handing Toby my grandfather's coat.

"If anyone sees you, just say I've hired you to fix some gaps in the barn," my father added. Which was a perfectly reasonable explanation.

But everything felt a little too easy to me as I headed off to bed.

When I woke, I knew I'd overslept. The light was late-morning bright and the house quiet. I hurried down to the kitchen where I found my grandmother, cutting butternut squash in half and laying them facedown on a baking sheet.

"What's wrong?" I said.

"Nothing at all," she said, smiling. "Your mother decided that you deserved to sleep a little longer."

It was awkward, not knowing what she knew or what I could safely say. The truth was so tightly braided with secrets that I could not easily say anything without saying too much. So I simply sat down to my cereal and waited for the day to unfold.

"Well, look who's up," my mother said as she came in the door, a basket of eggs in her hand. She tied on an apron and said, "Scrambled or fried?"

"I already had some cereal."

"Then go on and get ready for school." But as she said it, she winked at me. "I'll be up in a minute."

I was still marveling over the wink when she came into my room and shut the door.

"Your father took care of Toby this morning," she said softly. "Gave him breakfast." She sat down on the edge of my bed while I got dressed. "When he got back, he told me some things." She patted the bed next to her. "Annabelle, come sit for a minute."

When I did, she took a moment to choose her words. "Annabelle, your father thinks that Toby may be a little . . . confused."

"About what?"

"You know we've always thought he was odd. You did, too, I'm sure. Walking all day but going nowhere. Not talking unless he had to. Living in the smokehouse when he might have lived somewhere better."

"But I thought you liked him."

"I do," she said. "I always have. I'm sure he went through horrible things that made him the way he is, and I'll always help him if I can. But last night, in those clean clothes, with his hair and beard trimmed up, sitting at the table, and talking in complete sentences: He didn't seem odd anymore. But he *is* odd, Annabelle, and I don't want you to forget that."

"Did something happen in the barn this morning?"

She shook her head. "No, but your father spent some time with him and he reminded me, so I'm reminding you,

222

that you can't judge a book by its cover. Toby is confused. And you need to remember that, much as you like him."

I was baffled by all this talk of confusion and book covers. "I don't understand," I said. "You always said that people shouldn't be afraid of Toby just because he looked scary. And now you're saying that *I* should be afraid of Toby, even though he went down that well to get Betty, just because he looks *good*?"

My mother stared at me, still as a post. "Annabelle, I didn't say you should be afraid of him." She looked at her hands in her lap and sighed. "I'm just worried about you spending time alone with a man we really don't know all that well, who is, by all accounts, *odd*. Annabelle, he simply *is*."

"But—"

"Annabelle, you know how he carries those guns all the time?"

"Yes. So?"

"Your father had a look at them. Annabelle, only one of those guns works. The other two are ruined. They aren't good for anything. But he's carried them around for years, regardless, heavy as they are. Wouldn't you say that's a sign of confusion?"

I thought about the dreadful stories that Toby had told me. I remembered the baby only moments old.

I looked my mother full in the face. "I wouldn't say

that's a sign of confusion. I would say that's a sign of something that we don't understand. Toby has his reasons, and I don't think that makes him odd at all. Or if it does, then I'm odd, too, and so are you."

I got up and continued to get ready for school while my mother sat on the bed and watched me. Then she got up and left the room without another word.

School was different that day, for two reasons.

First, because I walked in to find myself the subject of a standing ovation. Even my brothers joined in, though they looked a little abashed about it. No one had ever clapped for me before, and I was sorry to be applauded now for something I might have done faster and better than I did.

In the second place, school was so much better without Betty, or Andy, for that matter, and I was not sorry about their absence. But it was also worse because Ruth was gone, too, and some of the littlest ones kept home by mothers who did not know Toby as I did and feared he might be lurking in the bushes, waiting to toss their babies down the nearest well.

We were no more than twenty, so Mrs. Taylor was able to spend plenty of time with us at the board in turns, doing sums and grammar.

It was during one of the arithmetic lessons that I began to realize what I should do next. The logic of the numbers was soothing, and it fired the nuts-and-bolts part of my tired brain.

If proving Toby innocent was the problem, then Andy was the answer.

He knew everything—who had thrown the rock, who had strung the taut-wire, why Betty had gone to Cobb Hollow—all of it.

If getting Andy to tell the truth was the problem, then I didn't know the answer.

But I remembered how much easier it was to tell my own secret when I realized my mother already knew part of it—that Jordan was really Toby. And once the cork was off the bottle, the rest of it flowed out.

If the answer was to pull the cork, then I needed to figure out how to convince Andy that we already knew the truth he had not yet told.

I spent the rest of the day thinking about that. And by the time school ended, I had the beginnings of an idea.

CHAPTER TWENTY-TWO

I needed some time to think about my new idea before I did anything about it.

For days I had popped from one problem to another like a pumpkin seed on a griddle. And I was tired of it.

Just weeks ago I'd begun to hunger for change, impatient with my life, much as I loved it. Somewhere, excitement waited for me like an uncut cake.

Now I wanted nothing more than to be still and thoughtful and quiet for just a little while.

The Turtle Stone was not far from the schoolhouse. Deer traveling the path out of Wolf Hollow had beaten other narrow trails that led to the fern beds they loved.

I took the first of these, once again grateful that Betty was not waiting for me. I wondered if I should feel guilty about that, but I didn't. I could have hurried more to find her, but I hadn't put her down that well. She'd done that all by herself.

I was truly alone. My brothers were long gone. And all the birds and small animals were hiding in plain sight, waiting to discover my intentions.

I had none.

The Turtle Stone sat at the center of the clearing like a great moon in a galaxy of yellow maple stars. It was a beautiful thing with quartz veins running deep and clear through its hard, reddish shell. We had long wondered about it—where it had come from, why it was the only one of its kind in these hills.

I'd been angry about a lot of Betty's nastiness, but when I saw the scars she'd made on the stone and remembered the reason for them, real fury overcame me.

I ran my hand over the stone, expecting some suggestion of softness. Instead, the stone itself told me a thing or two about age and resilience, and the trees at the edge of the clearing quietly concurred.

Who was I to worry about a stone that had been here since long before any of us, that would be here long after we all were gone?

I had come here to consider serious matters and how I might figure in the scheme of things. Important things.

Instead, the stone made me aware for the first time that my life, however long, would amount to nothing more than a flicker. Not even that. Not even a flicker. Not even a sigh.

As I made my way back through the woods, I thought of the men who had dug pits close by here. Maybe boys, too, not much older than I was right now.

I imagined those pits, the wolves trapped in them, snarling and whining for release. The bones they'd left behind. The unborn pups and their rose-petal ears.

I thought about Betty and her "gone" father and why she had intended Toby such harm.

The awful stories he'd told me, and the terrible softness of his scars.

And I decided that there might be things I would never understand, no matter how hard I tried. Though try I would.

And that there would be people who would never hear my one small voice, no matter what I had to say.

But then a better thought occurred, and this was the one I carried away with me that day: If my life was to be just a single note in an endless symphony, how could I not sound it out for as long and as loudly as I could?

When I got home, I found my mother and my grandmother in the sitting room, their laps full of mending.

I said my hellos and "Where are the boys?"

"Out in the haymow with Jordan," my mother said, giving me a look.

I kept my jaw from dropping. "With . . ."

"Jordan," my grandmother said, her eyes on her work. "Such a nice man to stay on and help your father patch up the barn."

"Can I go help, too?" I asked.

"For a while," my mother said. "Bring your brothers back with you when you come."

"Did you give Jordan some lunch?"

At which my mother looked up, smiling. "No, Annabelle. Your father asked him to help in the haymow all day, but we didn't invite him in at lunchtime."

My grandmother chuckled.

"I was just asking," I said.

"And I was just telling," my mother replied. "Now get out there so you can get back here to help with supper."

I followed the sound of hammering and boy-holler out to the barn. At the big upper doors to the threshing floor, I found my father and Toby patching a gap-toothed wall while my brothers swung to and fro from a knotted rope.

I guess it was jealousy I felt at the sight of them carrying on so well and easily without me.

"What kept you?" my father said. "The boys have been here a half hour or more."

"I spent some time at the Turtle Stone," I said.

My father and Toby both looked at me like the horses did when I disturbed their grazing.

"It's quiet there," I said. Which seemed to satisfy them both.

I looked over my shoulder at the boys, who were making more noise than crows over a hawk. "Did you hide the stuff up in the loft?"

My father nodded. "I buried the hair in the woods. We wrapped the guns in Toby's coat and stuck them under a bale of hay. The bedding, too. The camera's in his hat, behind the bales. And I told the boys to stay out of the loft."

Which was the most alarming thing he might have said. Telling the boys not to do something was like giving steak to a dog and telling him not to eat it.

"I have an idea," I said.

It amazed me when these two grown men put down their hammers at my four little words.

"Let's step outside," my father said. Toby and I followed him out through the big side doors. "What idea?"

I thought back for a moment to the thread that I'd followed at the schoolhouse. And the decision I'd made at the Turtle Stone: to use that thread to mend what I could.

"I think I know how to get Andy to admit that you're innocent, Toby," I said.

They waited.

"Andy and Betty saw you above them on the hill that day. They saw you up there with a camera."

"So?"

"So we just tell Andy that you took a picture of Betty throwing the rock."

Toby shook his head. "But I didn't. It happened too fast. And then they ducked back into the bushes. And all I got was a shot of the road down below. You. And Ruth, hurt."

"We know that, Toby," my father said. "We saw the picture. It made *you* look guilty. But Andy doesn't know that. He just knows you were up there on the hill with a camera. We'll tell him the pictures came back and one of them shows Betty throwing the rock. And if he thinks he's been caught in the biggest lie, he has no reason to lie about the rest of it."

"And you had no reason to push Betty down that well," I said to Toby.

"We need to go talk to Andy as soon as we can," I said to my father. "Take the constable with us so he can hear for himself what really happened."

But that's when the boys scattered our best-laid schemes like a fistful of birdseed.

We all turned as they raced out of the barn toward us.

"Look what we found!" they cried.

James held a black hat high in his fist.

Henry, a camera.

We stared at them, speechless.

"Toby's been in our barn," Henry said. "Maybe he's still around here, hiding." He suddenly lowered his voice. "Maybe he's still in the barn somewhere. Daddy, do you think he's still in the barn?"

What were we supposed to say?

We couldn't tell them that Toby was standing right in front of them. The boys were blabbermouths.

And we couldn't tell them not to say anything about what they'd found. They would see no earthly reason to keep such information from the police when there was a manhunt going on, whether they liked Toby or not.

"Where did you get those?" my father asked.

"In the loft," James said, dancing in place. "Behind some bales."

"Why would Toby leave his hat and his camera in our loft?" Henry said. "It doesn't make any sense. Unless he's still around here somewhere."

"How about we let the constable worry about that," my father said, taking the camera out of Henry's hands. "Now go on back to the house and wash up."

"But—"

"Get going," he said, relieving James of the hat. "We'll be along in a minute."

James made a face. "How come she doesn't have to go?"

"She'll be right behind you. Now git."

We watched the boys stomp away down the lane. Toby took off his gloves and rubbed his bad hand.

"This isn't good," my father said.

"I should go," Toby said.

"We need to get over to the Woodberrys' quick," I said.

"Annabelle, this is starting to feel like a mare's nest," my father said. "I think we should tell everything to the constable and let him deal with Andy."

"And if that doesn't work?"

We spent a moment in thought.

"I suppose you can stay in hiding, Toby, while we try it," my father said. "If Andy doesn't fess up, you can take off."

"And walk straight into a manhunt," I said.

Toby shrugged. "I walk quietly."

"You're not walking anywhere yet," my father said.

"What harm would it do to talk to Andy?" I said. "We can go right now, tell him there's a picture of him and Betty on the hill when Ruth got hurt, and see what he says."

"Which will mean trouble for you if he doesn't confess," Toby said. "You'll be telling lies to get him to tell the truth. People will wonder why."

"Let them wonder," my father said. "We've defended you all along. It's not a stretch to think we still might try to help you out."

"Which raises the question," Toby said slowly. "Why did you defend me all along?"

My father tipped his head up in surprise. "Because you didn't do anything wrong," he said.

Toby considered that for a long moment, rubbing his scars, and I heard his stories butting at their lids.

When Toby finally straightened up and took the hat out of my father's hands, I knew what was coming.

"Thank you for what you've done." He said it mostly to me, though he avoided my eyes. "But this is a game I don't want to play anymore."

He put the hat on.

Instantly, Jordan was no more.

"What are you going to do?" I said, following him into the barn.

But he didn't answer me. Nor did he answer my father, who asked him to stay until we could clear things up. He didn't seem to hear us as he climbed the ladder to the loft.

"That man's so stubborn he could be a member of the family," I said.

"From your mother's side," my father said.

We watched as Toby climbed back down in his long black coat, his guns once again slung across his back.

"Toby, you can't just go off like this," I said. "It's not a game."

But he simply paused for a moment to hand my grandfather's coat to me and to give my father the gloves he'd been wearing.

"You're really leaving?" I said. "Just like that?"

But he didn't answer.

It was hard to believe, after everything we'd tried, but I realized that he truly meant to go.

"Your camera," my father said, holding it out to Toby, who refused it with a wave of his hand. What I could see of his face was as pale as I'd ever seen it.

Then he turned and left the barn, walked out across the back pasture, and disappeared into the woods.

CHAPTER TWENTY-THREE

The story might have ended there.

But Aunt Lily had something to say about what happened next.

"Why haven't you called the police, John?" she barked when she arrived home from the post office and heard what the boys had found in the loft. "Or at least the constable. That madman could still be around here, and I for one won't sleep until he's caught."

My father was sitting in the chair by the stove, doing nothing, while my grandmother and I set the table.

"Lily, he left the camera for us to find. It's our camera. He's long gone."

"And the hat?"

To which he had no answer.

"And have you been up to search the loft properly?"

My father shook his head.

"John! He could still be in that loft, hiding, or gone away just today after the boys were up there."

My grandmother, who had thus far stayed on the edges of things, finally said, "John, much as we have always liked Toby, I think Lily has a point."

"Thank you, Mother," Aunt Lily said. "I'm sure Sarah feels the same way."

My mother, busy at the stove, did not comment.

Aunt Lily waited, watching my father, but he remained in his chair, thoughtful.

"Well, if you won't do it, then I will," she finally said.

When I started to object, my father held up his hand. "Let it be, Annabelle."

We heard her from the other room, telling Mrs. Gribble to put the call through, speaking with someone in the barracks in Pittsburgh, telling them to hurry up. And to bring the hounds.

I hadn't thought of hounds looking for Toby. I'd only thought of them hunting for Betty.

My father and I shared a look. In it, I could see that he realized what I did: that there were fresh trails all over the place. Not just around the well in Cobb Hollow. Not just in our barn. But in our truck. And straight into this kitchen, to that chair right there.

When Aunt Lily returned from her call, she said, "Officer Coleman will be here tonight. More men in the morning, if he says so." She looked sated.

"Then you can feed them, Lily," my mother snapped. "And clean up after them."

"Which I would be happy to do if I didn't have a job of my own," Aunt Lily said, sitting down at her place. "Sarah, I would think you'd be the one most concerned with the welfare of your children. More worried than any of us."

My mother pulled a roast out of the oven and put it down too hard on top of the stove.

"I'm plenty worried," she said. "Don't imagine for a minute that I'm not."

The boys had arrived at the prospect of imminent supper and talk of the police coming soon.

"Are they going to kill Toby?" James asked. He sounded afraid, and I was glad for that.

"Oh, hush now," Aunt Lily said, flapping her hand impatiently. "Nobody said anything about killing."

"Maybe not," my mother said. "But men with guns are coming after a man with guns. What do you think is going to happen?"

"They'll catch him!" Aunt Lily exclaimed, as if she were talking to a cluster of idiots. "For pity's sake, this isn't Germany. Nobody's going to shoot anybody unless they have to."

My grandfather came in from the front porch where he often sat the evenings, watching the light go. "What's all this about Germans and shooting people?" he said as he took his place at the head of the table.

"Nothing, Father," Aunt Lily said. "Just foolishness. Officer Coleman is coming back to make sure Toby's not hiding out around here. That's all."

"Because the boys found his hat in the barn?"

Aunt Lily nodded.

"Sounds a little thin to me," he said. "But I'm not the one who lost an eye. And I'm not the one who was down that well."

"This isn't fair," I muttered, but I knew I had nothing more to say about any of it.

"I heard that Jordan stayed to help fix the barn," Aunt Lily said, a little of that odd music in her voice. "But not for supper?"

It amazed me that we'd forgotten about that part of things. That there had ever been a Jordan, if only for a while.

"He had to get back," my father said. "But he said to tell you good-bye."

Aunt Lily smiled like a girl.

"He seemed like a very nice man," she said.

"He was," I said, a little too loudly.

Everyone looked at me.

"What? He was a nice man." I busied myself with a loose button on my cuff.

"So where is the hat?" Aunt Lily asked.

Silence.

"What hat?" my father said, his Adam's apple working.

She looked from my father, to me, to my brothers.

Henry shrugged. "We gave it to Daddy."

"Oh, that hat," my father said. "I left it out in the barn. It isn't the cleanest hat in the world."

"I should think not," Aunt Lily said.

"All right, enough," my mother said. "It's time for supper. And I don't want to hear one more word about Toby or his hat or troopers or bloodhounds or anything else. Do you hear me?"

We did.

We all tucked up to the table.

Aunt Lily said grace.

The food was good and I ate it, though I didn't feel any less hollow as a result.

"What's the news about Betty?" Aunt Lily asked.

"She's still not talking much," my mother said. "The gangrene wasn't so bad that she had to lose the toe, but she's a mess. That infection in her shoulder isn't getting

240

any better, in fact they fear it's worse, and she has a pretty high fever, so they're keeping her in the hospital." My mother had been nurse to all of us through so many mishaps and sicknesses that not much fazed her, but I had to put down my fork.

"I wish we'd got to her sooner," I said.

My mother knew how I felt about Betty. "You're a good girl, Annabelle."

"What about me?" James said.

"You're a good girl, too," my father said.

To which James said, "Aw, Daddy," and made a face.

I should have laughed, as Henry did. But I couldn't.

After supper was over and the dishes done, I went out and sat on the back steps in a pool of porch light. No mosquitoes hunting me at this time of year, or bats hunting them. Nothing to rush me back inside, except the thought of Officer Coleman returning.

I didn't want to see him.

I didn't want to talk to him about Toby or Betty or anything else.

I hated the thought of my parents having to sit at our kitchen table and lie to a policeman.

And I certainly didn't want to watch him search the barn.

But thinking about that reminded me of all the things I'd taken out there.

And what might be up in the hayloft still.

I ticked them off on my fingers.

My father had retrieved the Mason jars and the bedding, my mother's scissors, and the towel and soap and such. He'd buried Toby's old clothes in the burn barrel, under a month of ashes.

Toby had left the camera with us.

Given back my grandfather's coat and gloves.

Taken his guns.

But I was forgetting something. A stray spoon? A jam jar?

And then I remembered.

Treasure Island was still out in the barn.

If they found it, I could say I'd been reading it myself in the loft. Better, though, if they never found it at all.

I knew my way well enough without a lantern or a flashlight, and I was getting pretty good at running around in the dark, so I took off without a second thought.

The dogs in the woodshed woofed at me but didn't bother to leave their beds. The hens were all sleeping soundly in their nests as I hurried past. A leaf or two fell through the dark air, but I was not spooked. Nor was I slowed by the lack of moon.

"Hey, Bill," I said as I slipped into the barn through the stable gate. "Hey, Dinah."

I mooed quietly at the cows as I slipped by, just to let them know it was me, and then flew up the stairs and onto the threshing floor.

And paused.

I opened my mouth so I could hear better.

Something.

The barn creaked the way old barns do.

Something else.

A mouse scritched through the hay litter somewhere close by.

"Hello?" I whisper-called.

A stem of hay drifted down from above.

In the loft, a shape.

"Toby? Is that you?"

I hoped it was. I hoped it wasn't. But when he said my name I was more relieved than anything.

"Good grief, Toby, what are you doing back here?" I scrambled up the ladder into the loft and shepherded him away from the edge. "You scared me half to death. Are you back for good? Are you going to stay after all?"

He was wearing his coat and hat and, especially in the darkness, once again looked like something out of a tall tale.

"Not for good," he said. "Just for a minute."

"Just for a minute?" I was half baffled, half disappointed, as I seemed to be nearly all the time now. If he had come back, why was he leaving again? "Did you forget something?"

He nodded. "I did," he said.

"What? Your knife?" I remembered him handing it to my father for safekeeping before he went down the well.

"No. I have my knife."

"Do you want the camera? Toby, it's your camera. I can get it for you, quick, before the trooper gets here."

At which he drew himself up. "You called the police?"

"Of course not," I said, and I could hear the hurt in my own voice. "Do you think I would do that?"

He shook his head.

"My aunt Lily did when my blabbermouth brothers told her what they'd found."

Toby sat down on a hay bale and took off his hat.

"So they're coming." It wasn't a question.

"Just the trooper who was here before. But, Toby, you have to become Jordan again or you have to get out of here. He's coming to search the barn before he decides whether to look harder tomorrow, with more men. And bloodhounds."

Toby rubbed his bad hand. "And bloodhounds." He twisted a crick out of his neck.

244

I sighed. "I guess *they'd* know you, no matter what your name is."

"They would," he said. "They can track through water. Flood, even. Follow someone who's being carried."

"I didn't know that. And I wish they couldn't, though I don't think I could carry you either way. But if they're coming at all, they won't be here until morning, so you've still got time to get out of here. Find someone to give you a ride until you're far away. I can fetch my grandpap's coat again. And his gloves. Someone will give you a ride, I know they will."

Toby held up both hands. "Annabelle, stop."

I stopped.

He dropped his hands into his lap.

And I realized that he had never answered my question.

"If it wasn't for your knife," I said, "what did you come back for?"

I wished I could see his face better in the dark.

"When I left here, I meant to go straight west," he said. "And I started that way, for a mile or two. But it was all too quick."

He tipped his head back and swallowed hard. "I kept thinking about what I was leaving behind. So I turned around and walked to the smokehouse. To get some pictures," he said. "It was hard, both choosing them and working them off the wall." He stopped abruptly and dragged the back of his hand across his forehead.

"And then I came back here to say good-bye, Annabelle. It was rude to leave the way I did."

I liked that he had come all the way back to say a proper good-bye. But I didn't like the idea that he'd thought it rude.

"You don't need to feel obliged," I said, looking at my feet.

He held up a hand again. "I don't. I don't feel that way." He sighed. Gained his feet. Put his hat back on. Shifted his guns higher on his shoulder. "Annabelle, I would have liked a daughter like you," he said.

He put out his hand and I shook it, as if we'd made a pact.

Then he climbed down the ladder, crossed the threshing floor, and walked out through the big open doors.

Two things struck me as I stood in that loft and tried to remember what I'd come for.

One was that Toby had not said good-bye after all, and nor had I.

The second was that he carried only two guns.

I had never once seen him without three.

I remembered what my father had discovered: that only one of those guns still worked, the other two long past firing.

Toby had never really said why he carried all those heavy guns and had for years and years.

But I knew. Toby carried those guns because they were heavy.

I just didn't know why he had suddenly decided to lighten his load.

Treasure Island was waiting for me back behind the bales.

I spent a moment there, crying just long enough so I could breathe again, then I opened the hatch shutters wider and leaned out over the pasture.

I couldn't see to any great distance, but Toby was darker than the pasture grass, and I thought I saw him as he entered the woods. Or maybe I didn't.

Either way, he was gone, and I didn't expect to see him again.

I closed the shutters, tucked the book under my arm, and left the loft, the barn, heading home.

CHAPTER TWENTY-FOUR

"Hey," Henry said when he heard me come in through the mudroom door and saw what was in my hand. "That's my *Treasure Island*."

"Yes, it is," I said, handing it over.

He looked at it front and back. "What were you doing with it? Outside? In the dark?"

"I was reading to the dogs," I said, taking off my boots. "They especially liked the part where Black Dog comes looking for Bones."

"Very funny, Annabelle."

James had come out to the mudroom to investigate the possibility of something more interesting than *Cavalcade of America*, which my parents listened to through the cold months. The radio warbled away from the sitting room.

"Hey, that's my *Treasure Island*," James said, and in an instant they were tussling over the old book.

"You two make a fine pair," I said, edging past them. But I stopped when something fluttered from the pages and landed at my feet.

"What's that?" James said.

"A note from the dogs," I replied, slipping it into my pocket. "It says *Go to bed*."

"You're a riot," Henry said.

"*You* go to bed," James said.

"I think I will," I said.

After I brushed my teeth and washed my face, I spent a moment at the bathroom mirror. It was amazing, but I looked just the same as always.

"Good night," I said to my parents, grandparents, even Aunt Lily, who considered *Cavalcade of America* "an example of fine programming." Not like Red Skelton or *The Shadow*, though she sometimes sat in the kitchen at the end of the table nearest the sitting room when we listened to such "trash."

Safe in my room, I pulled from my pocket the picture that had fallen out of the book and studied it in the light from my bedside lamp.

The photograph was marbled with rough handling and shadows, but I could still see the sunstruck surface of a fishing hole as if I were looking down from the bridge above it.

I wasn't sure at first why Toby would have taken a picture of still water, or why he would have left such a picture for me to find.

But when I flattened it out on the tabletop and tipped it just so in the lamplight, I could see a vague reflection in the water, of the man with the camera on the bridge.

A self-portrait. The kind Toby would permit himself. How he looked, but secondhand, transformed by the water.

There was nothing on the back but the scar from where he'd pulled it off the smokehouse wall. Perhaps, if he'd had a pen, he might have written something.

As I tucked the photograph under my mattress, I heard a car crunching on the gravel in the lane. A door slamming. After a moment, someone knocking at the door.

Officer Coleman had arrived.

The house trembled with a migration to the mudroom door, the entrance of the big trooper, the excitement of my brothers, who must have forgotten, in the fray, that Toby had never done them any harm.

I hoped they would remember soon.

My bedroom window did not face toward the barn, so I was spared the temptation to watch as the trooper followed the beam of his spotlight in that direction, my father surely with him.

It took me a long time to fall asleep, but they had not yet returned before I did.

I slept so long and hard that when my mother woke me the next morning I was a stranger to myself. Whatever I had dreamed had taken me out of my life, and I spent a long moment coming back.

"You sure were tired," my mother said as my eyes cleared.

"I guess I was." I yawned loudly and stretched my arms over my head. "Do I have to go to school today?"

She picked up a stray sock from the floor and tossed it in my hamper. "I would think you'd be happy to get back to school."

"I will, when all this is over."

"It is over, Annabelle. For you. You won't want to be part of what comes next."

I didn't like the sound of that.

My mother sat down on the edge of my bed.

"What's going on?" I said.

"Officer Coleman checked the barn. He didn't find anything."

"Of course not. Toby's long gone." I had not told her

about his return, and I wasn't sure I ever would. With his picture under where I lay, I felt a little like the princess and the pea.

"Yes, but then Officer Coleman went down to the smokehouse to have another look around. And he did find something there."

I remembered that Toby had gone back to get his photographs.

"He left one of his guns behind. And it definitely wasn't there when Officer Coleman looked the first time, after Betty went missing."

I sat up.

"But here's the really odd part, Annabelle. The gun he left behind is a working gun, still loaded. The only good one Toby had. He took the other two broken ones, but he left the one that worked. Which makes no sense at all."

I wondered if he was afraid that he'd use it if they caught up with him. Or maybe he was just laying down part of his load.

I didn't believe in either answer. But I didn't have a third.

My mother was watching me curiously.

I rubbed the sleep from my eyes. "Did he leave anything else?"

"No. In fact, he took something. Photographs from his walls."

"That part makes sense."

She worried the edge of my blanket. "So now they know that he was in our barn at some point, because he left his camera and his hat there. Which, by the way, is another problem, since the hat wasn't in the barn anymore when they searched it last night." My mother ran her hands through her hair. "This is crazy, Annabelle. It's getting harder and harder to remember what we're supposed to know and what we're not."

"Why do you think I went to bed before Officer Coleman got here last night?"

She nodded. "I feel sorry for your father. He had to go out to the barn and act surprised that the hat wasn't where he'd left it. So now Officer Coleman is convinced that Toby's still right close by. And disturbed. And dangerous."

"But we know he's not," I said.

"We do. Which is why your father told Officer Coleman that Toby's other two guns are broken, so they wouldn't consider him armed."

"And shoot him," I said. I lay back down. "I hope he's miles from here by now."

"So do I. But they'll have bloodhounds." She didn't need to say anything else.

I pictured the dogs straining against their leashes, braying frantically, as they dragged their handlers through the woods.

"You're right," I said. "I do want to go to school."

My mother sighed. "Annabelle, I wish you could. But Officer Coleman has issued an order that everyone stay inside with their doors locked until Toby's found."

I sat up again. "What?"

"They don't want anyone to get hurt, by Toby or by accident. And they don't want him to have anywhere to hide."

"They can't lock every henhouse and oil shack, can they?"

"No, but they're not worried that Toby will take a bunch of chickens hostage."

"Hostage?" I scrambled out of bed. "They're the ones who are crazy. Mother, this all started because Betty lied about Toby hurting Ruth. And then about him pushing her down the well. Everyone's acting on her say-so. That's just not right. You know it's not."

"Annabelle, you can stand there in your nightie and make all the proclamations you want, but I don't see what we can do. It's out of our hands. Betty's not going to change her story. Why should she? Everyone thinks she's the victim. And I really can't blame them. She looks like one. And Toby looks like a villain, whether he is or not."

"So we just have to sit here in the house with the doors locked and wait for them to catch him?"

"I'm afraid so. Women and children inside. Men in the hunt."

I didn't know if I could take one more lousy surprise.

"Men in the hunt? You mean Daddy has to go hunt for Toby?"

My mother nodded. "He doesn't really have to. But he's the one who insisted that Toby's not armed. Dangerous, maybe, but not like he would be if he had a good gun. So they're asking any grown man to join in. We know these woods better than the troopers do, and the hounds are going to have a lot to sort out before they get it right. So in the meantime, it's a few policemen and a volunteer army, with whistles instead of guns. Nobody wants a shooting. And nobody wants Toby to get his hands on a proper weapon."

"Whistles?"

"So they can let the others know if they see him."

I tried to picture it. A bunch of farmers with whistles.

I was sure at least a few of them would arm themselves with something more, no matter what the trooper said.

Every year, some deer hunter shot his buddy by mistake, so I found it easy to imagine how a hunt like this might end.

"I'm glad that James and Henry are too young to join in," I said. "And boys like Andy, who would shoot anything that moved."

"And your grandpap, too old for anything but sitting in his truck with a thermos of coffee."

I pulled some pants and a sweater from my closet.

"Maybe they should put Aunt Lily on a leash and let her snuffle one of Toby's gloves."

"Annabelle, hush," my mother said, trying not to smile.

And I did hush then, to listen to the echo of what I'd just said.

"You know . . . we should hide Grandpap's coat. The one Toby wore. And the gloves, too. They'll smell just like him."

This time my mother did smile. "You think the bloodhounds are going to be in our mudroom?"

I shrugged. "Who knows? They might. A bloodhound can track through water," I said. "Even a flood. And it can pick up the trail of someone who's not even touching the ground, being carried by someone else."

"How do you know that?"

"Toby told me."

My mother frowned. "I wonder how he knew that."

"I have no idea, but he was in our kitchen just yesterday, so there's a trail from his smokehouse, to the barn, to the house and back, and then off into the woods."

My mother stood up. "Good grief," she said. "This gets better and better."

Neither of us said anything more as I got dressed. Brushed my hair. Began to make my bed. "They'll figure it out," I finally said. "They'll figure out that Toby was Jordan."

"You think so?" My mother straightened out my bedspread. "I suppose they will. If the hounds come to our door. But the freshest trail is from the barn and away, into the woods. They shouldn't come near the house."

"I'm still going to hide Grandpap's coat and gloves up here in my closet."

"All right," she said. "I suppose it won't do any harm."

And we both went downstairs to start one of the oddest days we'd ever spent, locked inside the house like prisoners ourselves.

CHAPTER TWENTY-FIVE

Betty Glengarry died at 10:18 that morning.

We didn't know about it for another hour.

Henry was the one who answered the telephone.

"It's Mrs. Gribble," he said, holding out the receiver to my mother.

My mother took the phone, her hand over the mouthpiece. "What does she want?"

"I don't know," Henry said. "Maybe she has a call for you but didn't want to put it straight through."

My mother put the receiver to her ear and leaned into the mouthpiece. "Hello, Annie?"

I could hear Mrs. Gribble, but not what she said. Just a babble, louder than usual, urgent, but not eager, the way she usually sounded when she had news.

My mother listened for a moment before suddenly gasping, her free hand flying to her cheek.

"Oh no," she said. "But how can that be? Oh, the poor thing. How is that possible?"

My mother wasn't a crier and she didn't cry now, but the look on her face was worse than tears.

I thought this was news that Toby had been killed.

I felt hot and terribly cold at the same time. Henry stood close beside me. He smelled like maple syrup and dog. I fiercely wanted to trade places with him.

"I'll tell him," my mother said, her voice breaking. "He and John are out with the hounds, but I'll tell him when I see him. I will, Annie. Thank you for letting us know. Good-bye."

My mother slowly hung the receiver back on its hook.

"Is he dead?" I asked.

"No," she said, turning to look at me. "Betty is. She died of infection. It spread everywhere and they couldn't stop it."

She sat down in the nearest chair.

Henry inched closer to me. I could hear him breathing.

"Hey," James called, galloping in from the mudroom where he'd been making a saber out of cardboard. "You wanna play pirates with me, Henry?"

"Sure. In a minute," Henry said. "But let's go find

Grandma first. I think she needs us to help her with something."

He gave me a long look, as if he were seeing me for the first time, and then he left the room, James trailing him like a noisy shadow. "Like what?" James said. "Does she need us to carry something? Henry, does she want us to carry something?"

The boy-sound grew distant.

I sat on the floor at my mother's feet and laid my head in her lap.

She stroked my hair as if I were a cat.

One of us was trembling. Maybe both.

"I could've found her faster," I said.

My mother's hand went still.

"Don't you dare do that," she said sternly.

She pushed my head off her lap and leaned down to look straight into my face.

"Do you think you're God?" she said impatiently. "Do you think you control things? Well, you do not. And it's arrogant to think that you do."

I was so surprised that I had nothing to say.

"Betty's dead, and that's terrible. *Terrible.* But you didn't do it, Annabelle."

She sat back. "In fact, if you hadn't led the way to that well she'd have died down there, alone and afraid. And we might never have found her at all."

I pictured Betty in the dark, cold, terrifying well, badly hurt. And dying, all by herself.

I pictured someone coming upon that well, years later, and filling it in with earth, burying her old bones deep in that accidental crypt.

"Come here," my mother said, opening her arms.

She was warm.

"Sometimes things come out right," she said. "Sometimes they don't."

I heard an echo of Toby in her voice. Something he had once said. Something about guilt or blame.

My grandmother did cry when she heard the news. It didn't matter that she hadn't known Betty.

I cried, too, the sight and sound of her tears spurring my own.

James didn't cry. When he heard that Betty had died, he laughed instead.

"Don't be silly," he said, waving his saber over his head.

It took my mother some time to convince him, and then he became very serious and went with Henry to make an "I'm sorry" card for the Glengarrys.

As he was leaving the room, Henry turned in the doorway. "Do you want to come with us?" he asked me.

The way he said it, the way he looked at me, took me aback. "I'll be up in a minute," I said.

"Annie Gribble asked me to tell the constable about Betty if I see him," my mother said.

"You can be sure everyone in the county will know it before he does," my grandmother said, drying her eyes. "Annie will see to that."

"She called it 'murder,'" my mother said quietly.

My grandmother cleared the tears from her throat. "That's exactly what it is," she said. "If Toby pushed that poor girl down a well, that's exactly what it is."

I clung to the *if* with all my might, but few people were as patient as my grandmother.

She might be willing to wait for certainty, but I doubted that the constable would be, or the police either, to say nothing of the Glengarrys.

If helping Toby had been important before, it was more so now. They would shoot him. Or, if they didn't, they would cuff him to an electric chair and cook the life out of him.

I prayed that he had let go of those old guns finally, tossed away his coat and hat, borrowed others from an unlocked house, and made his way to a road where a kind trucker might pick him up and take him to Ohio, maybe farther, before setting him down into a new life.

But I didn't think he'd done that.

I wasn't sure he'd even left these hills yet. He hadn't

seemed at all afraid. Just sorry to be blamed for what he hadn't done and weary with the burden of what he had, but not inclined to do much about either. Perhaps he was convinced that there was nothing he could do.

I felt like I was suffocating.

I paced from window to window, like James did every Christmas Eve, seeing nothing but his own reflection in the darkened glass but sure, nonetheless, that Santa Claus was out there somewhere, winging his way toward our farm.

I watched instead for farmers with whistles, or policemen with guns, but I didn't see anyone.

The horses in the pasture, like guardsmen, were the first to know that something was coming. They lifted their heads sharply, both at once, and stared into the woods leading down toward Cobb Hollow.

We heard the dogs, too, even through the locked doors and windows, long before we saw them. But it was our dogs making all the noise.

The bloodhounds, just two of them, were all business as they came into view, their long, droopy faces sweeping the ground ahead of them, one of them up from below the kitchen garden, the other across the horse pasture.

"They're coming this way," my grandmother said from the mudroom window. "And John is with them."

My grandfather's coat and gloves were already up in my closet.

I would smell like them, I realized. I would smell like Toby to those hounds. At least I hoped I did. I nearly smiled at the thought. Let them come on in. Who would believe a dog that thought I was a crazy woodsman?

Still, I was relieved to see the handlers tying the hounds up to the laundry posts.

"Sarah, you'd better put some more coffee on," my grandmother called over her shoulder. "We're about to have company."

The handlers were as quiet as their dogs—said very little, in fact, and softly when they did—and they acted much the same, looking around the kitchen curiously, from floor to ceiling, stopping often to zoom in on a detail they found of interest.

When my brothers came down to the kitchen, the handlers looked at them as if they were rabbits. James ducked back under the table, pulling on Henry's pant leg, whispering, "Come on, matey," but Henry sat next to me instead.

I looked at him curiously. He looked back at me, unsmiling.

My father and Constable Oleska had come in with the dog handlers.

"We decided to wait here for the others to catch up before we go back out," the constable said. "We already scoured the area around the smokehouse. So much scent there that we went in circles, but the dogs finally decided on this direction."

The men didn't bother to take off their coats.

"Sit down," my mother said. "We have some news."

When he heard that Betty had died, the constable said, "Lord God," and put his head in his hands.

The dog handlers barely noticed. They must have been through such things a hundred times. Missing children. Criminals on the run. After a while, they must have become as matter-of-fact as their dogs, intent only on the chase.

They had been denied the chance to find a missing girl. They would do what they could to find her killer.

My father looked from my mother to me, his eyes full of questions. *What should we do now? How are we supposed to know what to do now?*

I wasn't sure, either. But I knew I couldn't spend one more minute doing nothing. I knew I couldn't grow up and live a long life with the knowledge that I had not done what I could. Right now. Before it once again made no difference.

I slipped out of the kitchen and into the sitting room, leaving the rest of them to sort out their next steps.

Mine were clear, but I sat quietly for a while and went through them in my head, watching myself do and say the only things I could think to do or say.

I didn't see how I could make things any worse than they were.

I carefully shut the door between the kitchen and the sitting room.

I picked up the telephone receiver and turned the crank as quietly as I could.

"Mrs. Gribble?" I said softly into the mouthpiece.

"Sarah?"

"No, it's Annabelle, Mrs. Gribble. Can you put me through to the Woodberrys please? It's very important." I knew that would whet her appetite.

"Annabelle, does your mother know you're using the telephone?"

"Of course," I said. "Do you want to speak with her? She's helping my grandma with some chores right now, but I can get her if you want. Only we need to hurry. This is really important."

I held my breath.

"That's all right," she said, and I could hear the anticipation in her voice. "Which Woodberry did you want?"

I hadn't thought about such a question. "The ones that have an Andy," I said.

"They all have Andys," she said, losing patience.

"The young Andy. The one who goes to school with me."

For once, I was glad that Mrs. Gribble made it her business to know everything about everyone in these hills.

She put the call through.

When Mrs. Woodberry answered, I willed Mrs. Gribble to stay on the line.

"Mrs. Woodberry, this is Annabelle McBride," I said. "May I please speak with Andy for a minute?"

"Well, if you're calling to tell him about Betty, he already knows," she said. "She sure was a sweet thing, wasn't she? What an awful shame."

"No, it's not about that," I said. Though it was.

"All right, let me get him," she said, putting the receiver on top of the phone with a clunk.

I was grateful for the police order to stay inside. Surely, Andy was somewhere nearby.

I could hear her calling for him. Once. Twice.

And then, after a minute, he said, "Hello?" in a flat, gray voice.

I had intended to jump right in, but at the sound of him I softened. "Andy, this is Annabelle. I'm so sorry about Betty."

Silence on the line. And then, "I am, too," which surprised me, though I had never doubted his odd affection for her. The sorrow in his voice nearly stopped me in my tracks.

"I wanted to ask you something," I said slowly, pausing to find my way back to where I needed to be. "We just got back some pictures Toby took, and one of them has Betty in it." Her name stopped me. This was harder than I had thought it would be.

"What does that have to do with me?" Andy said. He sounded both curious and worried, as I could easily imagine he was.

"It was a picture of you and Betty, on the hill across from the schoolhouse. Betty was throwing a rock at Mr. Ansel down below."

If Mrs. Gribble was listening, I knew she wouldn't leave now, no matter how many or how bright the lights on her switchboard.

I could hear Andy breathing, but he didn't say a word.

"Telling the truth can't hurt Betty now," I said.

"Why do you care about that?" Andy said, clearly worried still but angry, too. "You can't punish her for throwing that stupid rock. She's already dead. What does it matter?"

There. That was the first part I needed Mrs. Gribble to hear. I let myself breathe.

"Because they think Toby killed her," I said. "That's why. And you know he didn't push her down that well."

"She said he did," Andy said, his voice harder than before. "When they got her to the hospital, she said he did."

"And she said he threw that rock, too, which was a lie. You just admitted it."

"*Because she was scared.* She didn't mean to hit Ruth."

I closed my eyes. *Please,* I thought. *Please be listening.*

"Andy, I know you cared about Betty. But you're the one who said she went down to the smokehouse to cause trouble, maybe burn Toby out. Why can't you admit that she fell down that well by accident?"

"What does it matter?" he said. "So what if she did? She's the one who's dead and he's off scot-free."

"But now they think he's a murderer!" I said, trying to keep my voice down. "And they're going to kill him."

"I hope they do," he said quietly. "I hope they kill him twice."

"Andy, you can't hope that."

He answered by hanging up.

A moment later, I heard Mrs. Gribble disconnect, too.

I replaced the receiver and sat down on the floor, shaking with exhaustion.

My mother came looking for me moments later. "Who were you talking to in here?" she said. "Annabelle, are you all right?"

"I don't feel good," I said. "Can I go lie down?"

She put her hand on my forehead. "You don't have a fever."

"I'm not sick," I said. "I just don't feel good."

"Go on, then." She reached out a hand to help me to my feet. "The men are headed back out with the hounds."

When I stood up, she put her arms around me and rested her chin on the top of my head.

"This will soon be over," she said softly. "One way or another."

CHAPTER TWENTY-SIX

It didn't take long for Mrs. Gribble to spread this second piece of news.

People often complained about her eavesdropping and swore they didn't listen to her gossip, but the stories she spread had always proven true (except one April Fool's Day when someone fed her a bogus tale about a wagon train of gypsies setting up camp in Bocktown), and she was widely regarded as the county crier.

By suppertime, everyone knew that Toby was not responsible for Ruth losing her eye. And there was now some doubt about whether he'd pushed Betty down the well. But doubt wasn't enough.

"A jury can have doubt if it wants to," the constable said. "But the police still have to find the man."

He sat in our kitchen with my father and grandfather, even James for once *at* the table instead of under it.

The dogs had led the search party into the barn and out again, across the pastures and around the house, up the lane and back down, into the woods and orchards, before finally setting a course away from our hills, west, toward Ohio, which was not so very far from here.

They'd followed the scent for a couple of miles, maybe more, before Officer Coleman declared this a certain trail unlikely to loop back.

"That's when he sent us home," my father said. "They're still on the trail and will stay on it until they're relieved by fresh dogs and men."

Constable Oleska looked worn-out and not at all sorry to be done with searching. "They're sure to catch up with Toby in a day or two, unless he hitches a ride."

"Do you think they'll go into Ohio after him?" my father said.

"Yes, I expect they will, or hand it over to the Ohio police. But when they hear Annie's latest bulletin—and they will, if they haven't already—they're apt to stand down a bit."

He turned to look at me. "I guess it's a good thing Mrs. Gribble listened in on that call you made to Andy," he said. He wasn't smiling, but he wasn't scolding, either. "Imagine her doing that."

"Imagine *you* doing that," my father said to me.

"Are you angry?" I was prepared for people to be angry with me, though it didn't matter as it once would have.

"Not angry," my father said.

"Not angry at all," my grandfather said. He smiled at me from his end of the table. "Gumption's a good thing, if you ask me."

"So is industry," my mother said as she slid a pan of pork chops into the oven. "Annabelle, those carrots aren't going to peel themselves."

"I'll do it," Henry said, rising from his chair. He didn't look at me as he took my customary place at the sink, but I knew he could see me anyway. We had the same hands. The same long fingers. The same way of holding a knife.

"How come Henry gets to help and I don't," James said.

"You're absolutely right." My mother handed him a saucepan. "You can start by putting a cup of milk into this pan."

Aunt Lily came home just then to the sight of Henry and James helping to get supper ready while I sat at the table with the men.

"Am I in the right house?" she said. She took off her coat and hung it in the mudroom closet. "Annabelle, have you lost the use of your legs?"

"Easy, Lily," my father said, as if she were a fractious horse. "It's been a long day."

"As if I don't know it. Do you have any idea how much mail comes through that post office? It's a wonder anything else gets done around here, with all the letters people write."

She helped herself to a cup of coffee and sat down at my mother's place.

I thought that she had somehow missed the news of Betty's death, so I told her. "Betty Glengarry died this morning, Aunt Lily."

"Which I heard from at least a dozen people today," she said. "I don't work in the Timbuktu post office, Annabelle. If there even is such a thing."

I wanted to throw something at her. "I thought you might not know."

"Why, because I'm not gasping and fainting like all the other ninnies?" She looked at me over her glasses. "The Lord works in mysterious ways, Annabelle. He has His reasons."

My grandmother came into the kitchen just in time to hear this. "Reasons for what?" she said.

"For taking Betty home."

My grandmother shook her head. "I don't know where you got such a hard heart, Lily."

"Not hard. But not soft, either. Plenty of those around here already."

I thought if I had to listen to Aunt Lily for one more minute I would turn to stone. "Since the boys are helping with supper, can I go up to my room for a while?"

"For a little while," my mother said. "I'll call you when I need you."

"I can set the table," James said.

"Of course you can," my grandmother cooed, ruffling his hair. "Whoever said you couldn't?"

From my bedroom, I could hear the others down below. The sound of pots and pans. Dishes and flatware. Voices. A chair scraping.

All of which had the effect of making me feel even more lonely.

Tricking Andy into a confession, knowing that the police might be more gentle with Toby if they caught him, did not help much.

From my closet, I took my grandfather's coat and slipped it on. There was room inside for two of me.

I lay down on my bed, drew my knees up into the coat, and fell sound asleep.

I didn't hear my mother call me down for supper.

I didn't hear her open my bedroom door, turn off my light.

I didn't feel her pull my bedspread up over me.

And I didn't wake later that night at the sound of the telephone ringing.

After such an early bedtime, I was up well before most everyone.

I found my mother in the kitchen, brewing coffee, but no one else. The world was dark beyond the windows.

I watched her for a moment. She looked different, not knowing that anyone was there, all of her facing inward, as I had on the path when Toby took my picture.

An inkling told me to go back to bed before she saw me.

Perhaps it was how sad she looked, though I couldn't see her face, that urged me to go away, quickly, so I could have another hour—maybe two—before I found out why.

I was still in my clothes from the day before, still wearing my grandfather's coat.

How silly I must have looked when she turned toward me, a mug of coffee in her hand, and stopped so suddenly that the coffee sloshed over the rim and onto the floor.

"Annabelle, you startled me," she said, reaching for a rag. "What are you doing up so early?"

"I couldn't sleep anymore." I sat down at the table. "Did they find Toby yet?"

"You heard the telephone ring?"

I shook my head, my heart shrinking. "Who called?"

My mother rinsed out the rag and sat across from me. She set her mug down carefully.

"The constable called," she said. "He had just heard from Officer Coleman, and he thought we'd want to know what happened."

I didn't know how beautiful my mother was until I saw her in that moment as she gathered herself to tell me that Toby was dead.

I held my hands inside the sleeves of my grandfather's coat while she told me that they had caught up with him just before the border into Ohio, sleeping under the Mahoning River bridge.

She told me that when the hounds reached him, they lay down in the leaves along the edge of the river and took no interest in the man himself, who stood up when the policemen called his name.

Perhaps, she said, he wanted to be standing when the next part came, because when they told him to lie down again on his face and put his hands behind him, he refused.

And when they pulled out their pistols and told him a second time, he slipped one of the long guns off his back, and they shot him.

"They didn't know that his gun was useless," she said quietly. "They didn't know anything about what had happened here. They only knew that they were supposed to catch a dangerous man and take him into custody."

I pushed the coat's long sleeves up my arms and dried my face with my hands.

"Why would he do that?" I said. "Grab his gun like that? It didn't even work. And Toby wouldn't have shot at them anyway. He just wouldn't."

My mother sighed. "I don't think so either," she said. "And I don't know why he did what he did. Except maybe he had had enough of this world, Annabelle."

"After all this time of living with how sad he was? He decided that he couldn't stay here anymore *now*? When he had us?"

My mother shook her head. "I don't know, Annabelle. But think about how it feels when your hands are so cold they go numb. How it's only when they start to thaw out that you realize how much they hurt."

I spent some time looking at my hands, thinking about his. "He said that he would've liked to have had a daughter like me."

My mother smiled. "Anybody would," she said.

I remembered the night I'd taken Toby to the barn for safekeeping. "Did you know that he was afraid of heights?"

She shook her head.

"But I shamed him into climbing the loft ladder,

and he never hesitated after that. Just did it, like it was nothing."

My mother got up and poured me a small cup of coffee with plenty of cream and sugar. "You knew him better than I thought you did."

"He knew me before I knew him."

And we drank our coffee in silence as the sun came in through the windows and all the colors with it.

CHAPTER TWENTY-SEVEN

I sat at the kitchen table and waited for my family to wake, one by one. Each of them in turn, right down to James, and especially Henry, told me how sorry they were that Toby had died.

Except Aunt Lily, who sat watching, drinking coffee in her pink flannel robe, and said, "I still don't understand how a man like that could be anything but terrifying to a girl like you."

I didn't answer her, but Henry did.

"She was his friend," he said, but Aunt Lily just snorted.

"And why are you wearing that coat?" she said. "It looks just like the one Jordan was wearing when he came to help find Betty."

My mother seemed about to say something, but she

looked at my father, he shook his head, and they both nodded to me as if to say, *Go ahead. It's all right.*

My grandfather leaned closer and then back with a nod. "That's my old coat," he said. "And it looks very fine on you, Annabelle. Maybe a bit too long in the sleeve."

I pulled the gloves from the right-hand pocket of the coat and put them on the table.

"And my favorite gloves," my grandfather said. "I've been looking for those."

"Jordan had gloves just like those, too," Aunt Lily said slowly. "I thought it was odd that he wore them to the dinner table that night."

Henry came over to examine them. "Not ones like them. He had these very ones," he said. "I saw that berry stain on the thumb when he was hammering up new planks in the barn. I remember it looked like Africa."

James was the only one at the table who found his breakfast more interesting than the gloves that lay quietly alongside my plate, waiting patiently to be worn again.

"But why do you have Jordan's gloves?" Aunt Lily said. "Did he forget them?"

"Lily, those are my gloves," my grandfather said. "And that's my coat. And what Jordan was doing with them I neither know nor care. Now pass me the sugar, Lily, and the cream, Annabelle, or I'll have to drink this coffee black."

Henry was staring at me. My parents watched in silence. My grandmother spread jam on a piece of toast. James stole a slice of bacon off Henry's plate, unnoticed.

"But why—" Aunt Lily began.

"That wasn't Jordan," Henry said, his eyes wide as an owl's. "That was Toby."

My grandfather put down his fork. "Who was Toby?"

"Jordan," Henry said. "He took off only one of his gloves. At the dinner table. So we wouldn't see his scars."

"Don't be ridiculous," Aunt Lily said, scowling into her coffee cup. "Jordan is a very nice man."

"Who came out of nowhere," my grandmother said thoughtfully. "Wearing that coat, and those gloves." She looked at me curiously. "Annabelle, why are you wearing that coat?"

I looked at my parents again and took the last step. "Because I was cold last night, up in my room, where I hid the coat so the bloodhounds wouldn't find it in the mudroom."

By now even James was paying attention. "Why would bloodhounds be in the mudroom, Annabelle? That's dumb."

"Because they were following Toby's scent," Henry said.

"Oh, for pity's sake," Aunt Lily said. "Toby has never been in this house. Not once. Or in your grandfather's coat, for that matter."

"Jordan was Toby," Henry said. "Wasn't he, Annabelle?"

I nodded. "Yes, he was, Henry. And you're right, Aunt Lily, he was a very nice man."

In the confusion that followed, I let my father answer the questions while Aunt Lily's face changed from white, to red, to white again.

I slipped my hands in the big pockets of my grandfather's coat and, as I watched her grapple with her revelations, made a fresh discovery of my own.

Toby, who knew such a great deal about shame, had left us something that had the power to shame even Aunt Lily.

I found it, cold and hard, in the bottom of the left-hand pocket. I tried to pull it out, but it was pinned to the lining.

"There's something in this pocket," I said, standing up.

Everybody stopped talking.

I unbuttoned the coat so I could work with both hands.

And unpinned what turned out to be a gold star with a face engraved on the middle, set inside a wreath. At the top was an eagle perched on a bar that had the word VALOR on it.

I turned it over.

"What did you call Toby?" I asked Aunt Lily slowly. "A monster? A madman?"

I handed the star to my father, who looked at it closely and read aloud what was engraved on the back. "'The Congress to Tobias Jordan.'" He looked up at me, as pale as Aunt Lily. "Annabelle, this is a Congressional Medal of Honor."

"Let me see that," Aunt Lily snapped. She scrutinized the medal, looking for a way out, but there was none. "Well, how were we supposed to know the man was a war hero?" she said, handing the medal on to my grandfather, who held it as if it were made of glass.

"He wasn't," I said. "He would have told you that himself if the police hadn't killed him last night."

I went to school that day, but I don't remember a single thing about it.

I'm sure much was made about Betty's death, and I'm sure that Benjamin was back in the seat that Andy had claimed for much of the month. I didn't expect to see him in school for some time. And I would never be afraid of him again.

I do remember that Henry waited for me in the schoolyard at the end of the day instead of running ahead with James.

"Do you want to walk with us?" he said.

I shook my head. "It's okay. I'm okay. You go on now. I'll see you at home."

In truth, I wouldn't have minded the company, especially that of a brother who seemed to regard me as an actual person now.

But I had somewhere to be, and I wanted to go there by myself.

There were only a couple of hours of light left on this short November day, and I had some distance to cover, but I paused along the path where Betty had first confronted me and had a word with her before I left. I told her that I was trying to forgive her and myself both, but I didn't know if I could, and she didn't answer in any event.

I went, then, to the place where the wolf pits had once been, and I spent some time there, as well.

But the wolves that had died there were silent, too. And it was only as I stood in that place, listening, that I realized I'd been hearing them for weeks now, translated.

I hoped that maybe they'd help me understand Toby's stories someday, if I was ever brave enough to unlid them again.

Toby's smokehouse was already beginning to miss him.

A spider had left an egg sac in a web above where he'd slept, and I pictured the hatchlings cascading down into his nest of pine boughs when the thaw came next spring.

There was raccoon sign in one corner, near the vent

for Toby's fire, and I knew I wouldn't be able to come back here again.

It took me a long time to free the remaining pictures from the walls.

That he had used tree sap suggested two things: He'd had nothing else to use, or he'd meant to stay here forever.

I cried over both answers.

I had brought a paring knife to slice the photographs free, warming the sap first by pressing my hands over each picture, but I still ruined the most stubborn of them.

The ones I took were wrinkled from the process, and most were thin where the backing paper had come away. If I held them up to the light, a part of each photograph seemed to glow. I liked that.

I left a few, partly so I could get home before dark but mostly because they belonged where they were. The deer napping in mayapples. A red fox after mice in the strawberry patch, the tip of its tail a white arrowhead.

The last one I took with me was of a hawk standing on the Turtle Stone. I nearly left it behind because it was so beautiful, but I took it because it was so beautiful.

I expected a scolding when I got home that evening. Instead, my mother said a simple hello and handed me an apron.

And when Henry came into the kitchen, looking relieved to see me there, I handed him the stack of photographs.

"Toby left these," I said. "If you want, the camera's in my bedroom. I loaded a fresh spool of film. We can take turns with it, spool by spool."

"What about me?" James said, prancing into the kitchen wearing a coonskin cap. Apparently, my grandmother had started to read him a new book, presumably about the Wild West.

"You can take some pictures, too," I said.

"Did Daniel Boone take pictures?"

"I doubt it," Henry said.

"Then I don't take pictures either," James said, galloping off into his own private wilderness.

Henry turned to me. "So the camera will be for just us," he said.

And the way he said it made me think I might be happy again soon.

Betty's was an odd funeral. The church was full, every pew, mostly with people who had never met Betty but knew her grandparents or had known her father growing up or had heard of her terrible death and wanted to send her off properly.

I recognized Betty's "gone" father from the picture in

her bedroom. He chose a seat apart from her mother, who sat in the front pew and wept into her hands.

I was sitting where I could see that his face was dry. But when we stood to sing "Nearer, My God, to Thee," he folded over in his seat and endlessly rubbed his eyes, his shoulders trembling.

Betty's grandfather had made her casket himself. Painted it white. I thought it was a shame to put it into the muddy hole they had dug for her. And it seemed too cruel to leave her there alone with no company but the flowers we had laid on top of her casket, mostly the last of the wild asters and goldenrod we'd managed to gather from the dying fields.

But leave her we did, every last one of us, though some more slowly than others. And when we passed by the graveyard the next day there was nothing but a raised bed of bare earth, strewn with tattered flowers and leaves, where Betty had last been.

Now that she was gone, Betty reminded me of the April cold snaps that kept my father up all night, feeding bonfires in the peach orchard to save the tender blossoms from freezing.

Some of them would survive to become fruit as good as anything on earth. Others would wither on the branch, killed by frost, wasted.

It seemed to me that Betty had been both the flower and the frost.

Toby's funeral was quite different.

We didn't have much money, but we had enough to bring Toby's body home and bury him, not in the churchyard but on top of the hill above Wolf Hollow, beneath a plain marker engraved with his name and the years of his life.

It had been easy to find out when Toby had been born— the army told us that, along with the fact that he had no living relatives—but we were the ones who told them when he had died.

They sent us a packet of information about what he'd done to earn the medal, but I had already heard his side of the story, and none of it mattered much now. Not to me.

We all gathered on the top of that hill after we'd laid Toby to rest. Mostly, we just stood silent, which seemed a fitting good-bye.

But Aunt Lily surprised me. "I regret passing judgment on that man," she said, looking not at his grave but away into the distance, as if he were somewhere else . . . which I suppose he was, though it didn't feel that way to me.

After a time, my grandparents made their way slowly back toward the house, Aunt Lily trailing along behind them.

My parents kissed me and went away, too.

"Come on, Annabelle," Henry said as the light began to fail. "Let's go."

But I wasn't quite ready to leave yet, so Henry stayed on, and James, who had scampered off a ways, came curiously back, the dogs with him, to lie in the grass by Toby's grave and comment at length on the clouds overhead.

And then we all went home.

From time to time, over the years after that, I sat on top of the hill alongside Toby's grave, looking out over Wolf Hollow, and told him about my life.

The hollow seemed to listen, too, and I often wondered about everything else it had heard over the centuries. The sound of men digging pits. The hopeless confusion of the wolves they had trapped. Perhaps one who had not been fooled by the scent of the bait, still on safe ground, pacing along the rim above, looking down into the pit at his doomed mates. Then retreating into the woods as the men came back in the morning with their guns.

I imagined him so torn between the need to fight and the urge to live that he felt as if he, too, were bleeding. And I could not help but think of the hollow as a dark place, no matter how bright its canopy, no matter how pretty the flowers that grew in its capricious light.

But Wolf Hollow was also where I learned to tell the truth in that year before I turned twelve: about things from which refuge was impossible. Wrong, even. No matter how tempting.

I told Toby as much, though I also said that I didn't blame him for fleeing the greater evils he'd known. And I thanked him for letting me try to right any number of wrongs, regardless of his own surrenders.

But the wind always swept my words away like cloud shadows, as if it mattered more that I said them, than who heard them.

And that was all right with me.

ACKNOWLEDGMENTS

I am grateful to many people for their help with *Wolf Hollow*. First among them is my mother, Mimi McConnell, whose wonderful stories of life on a farm in western Pennsylvania inspired this book. Her entire family, and the farm itself, figured greatly in my own life for decades and helped me create an authentic setting. My father, Ronald Wolk, and my sister Suzanne Wolk have been among my first and most perceptive readers. Their insight and encouragement have been invaluable. My sister Cally has always been in my corner, too, along with my husband, Richard, and our sons, Ryland and Cameron, who have made me a better writer, not only through their insights but also their support when the demands on my time and energy were great.

The members of my incredible writers' group—the Bass

River Revisionists—have been with me through thick and thin, and I will always be grateful to them for their keen brains and warm hearts, especially Julie Lariviere and Maureen Leveroni who first invited me to join their ranks, and Deirdre Callanan for devoting so much time and care to her own craft and to mine. I am blessed with a great colleague, Robert Nash, who has always understood that although I love the work we do together, my writing deserves time and attention, too. He has been a true friend.

I owe a debt, as well, to my former agent Dan Green, whose shift to nonfiction convinced him I'd be better off with different representation. He is a class act, as are Jodi Reamer, my superb agent at Writers House, and Julie Strauss-Gabel, my excellent editor. In fact, the entire Penguin Young Readers family has demonstrated an extraordinary commitment—both passionate and professional—to this book. I could not have asked for a better team. Finally, I am grateful to Annabelle for taking me into Wolf Hollow and showing me the way back out again. I'd like to be as brave as she is.